The Revelation

A NOVEL

The Revelation

A NOVEL

JEAN GRANT

Thomas Nelson Publishers

NASHVILLE

Published in Nashville, Tennessee, by Thomas Nelson, Inc., and distributed in Canada by Lawson Falle, Ltd., Cambridge, Ontario.

Scripture quotations are from the NEW KING JAMES VERSION of the Bible. Copyright © 1979, 1980, 1982, Thomas Nelson, Inc., Publishers.

Library of Congress Cataloging-in-Publication Data

Grant, Jean.
    The revelation / Jean Grant.
       p.   cm.
    ISBN 0-8407-3454-9 (pb)
    1. Tribulation (Christian eschatology)—Fiction.   I. Title.
PS3557.R2663R48   1992
813'.54—dc20   92-36948
                                            CIP

Printed in the United States of America
1 2 3 4 5 6 7 — 96 95 94 93 92

1

Pam Cristman stirred and awakened. The massive oak bed rocked, and the ranch house walls zigzagged crazily in the pale dawn. Pam shuddered involuntarily, then quickly brushed aside the horrible thought she had taken to bed with her a few hours before. It was only an earthquake. She was a native Californian and not about to be terrified by a little shaking.

David grunted and sleepily slapped an arm across her. "Earthquake?" he muttered, as a second tremor shook them to consciousness.

"Not big enough to do much damage around here," Pam commented. "But I hope it wasn't worse somewhere else." She fumbled for the bedside radio, but it responded only with static. "Whoops! That sounds like trouble." She tried to tune in another station, but without success.

"Power's off, Pam."

THE REVELATION

"I guess that's why I can't get anything on the radio. The local station's transmitter probably hasn't any power either, and our batteries are too weak to bring in anything from San Francisco."

"I sure hope that's all. They do keep predicting another big one, though." David pulled on his jeans and started outside. "I better check the livestock."

Pam gave the house a quick once-over in the dim dawn. Nothing was out of place in the kitchen cabinets or closets. The pears and applesauce and tomatoes she had canned last summer still stood in ordered ranks on the pantry shelves.

She knew she shouldn't tie up phone lines; but her sister, Sandy Peters, was in the South Bay, and Sandy was Pam's sister, mother, and best friend. Pam picked up the phone, but was not really surprised to find the line dead. That was the only thing she didn't like about living up here on their beautiful, isolated Mendocino County ranch. Phone lines and power lines went down on any excuse, and it might be days before she and David were in touch with the world again.

David came back into the room as Pam laid kindling on the glowing coals in the wood stove. His presence and the sudden tongues of bright flame drove the lonely chill from her heart and her body as they always did. "Did you find any problems outside, hon?" she asked. "There doesn't seem to be any damage in here."

"The cows were a little restless, but I went ahead with the milking and put them out to pasture. Are you sure the chimney's sound, since you've already stoked the stove?" He glanced quickly up the length of the stovepipe.

"Oh, I just didn't think. Oh, David." Her wide, dark eyes glistened with a hint of a tear.

"Hey, hon, don't look so scared. I don't think there's anything wrong. I'll just run upstairs and check out the attic to make sure. That's all."

"You'd think after two years up here I'd have more sense than to light a fire after an earthquake without checking the chimney," she apologized, as she followed him up the old, hand-carved staircase.

"So you're a city girl. That's one of the things I love about you." His blond head disappeared through the attic access hole, and he twisted a little to get his broad shoulders through the narrow space. "All's well," he echoed from above. "No smoke, no flame, no problem." He wriggled back out and down, a comforting grin on his young face.

"I am sorry. It was a stupid stunt."

"Oh, hush, Pam. There's no harm done and, from the looks of things outside, we're really going to need that fire."

Pam glanced out the window and was surprised to see massive thunderheads marshaled along the ridge of the Coast Range just west of them. "First an earthquake, and then one whale of a storm," she shuddered. "Not much of a beginning for our Thanksgiving weekend."

Pam had relished the stormy days last winter, days when David could not work outside from dawn to dusk building stock pens, fencing the rolling acres, and turning the peaty soil that had been untilled for a generation. On the nastiest days he had worked with her in the old redwood Victorian, sanding its worn plank floors, patching the holes in the plaster walls, building the deep shelves and cupboards that now held all their beloved books and her handmade pottery.

The worst of the restoration was behind them now. The sturdy farmhouse would hold out the wind and rain, and the ranch was self-sufficient even if snow closed the winding, narrow road to town for days at a time.

Pam reached out a slender hand and brushed an attic cobweb from David's hand-knit sweater. "Let it rain. You deserve a day off."

A tiny pinprick of fear still lurked in the back of her mind. Had the quake hit a major population center? Were there dead and injured people somewhere? And what about the war rumors from Israel?

Later, as David asked the Lord's blessing on their farm breakfast, he gave voice to Pam's concerns. "And, Lord, if there has been serious damage from this earthquake, bless your children in the midst of it and protect them from harm. And give wisdom to our diplomats as they strive to bring peace to your Holy Land. Amen."

The storm came up very quickly and it was the worst Pam and David had yet seen on the stormy ridge. High winds dropped branches from the second-growth oak and manzanita. Hail fell intermittently. "Winter seems to have arrived a little early this year. I'd better get the cows into shelter," David said, as he hauled his heavy windbreaker out of the closet.

"It might be quite a while before the power comes back on. I'll have some soup warm on the wood stove when you get back in." Pam stood on tiptoe, her black curls just brushing David's face; after two years of marriage they still kissed when they parted, even if for an hour.

Pam looked through the new, triple-paned windows of the old house. The storm was past enjoying now. Some of the hailstones were the size of Ping-Pong balls. And the phone and radio were both still silent.

She worried about her sister, Sandy, and Sandy's husband and children. They were coming up today from their home in San Jose to spend Thanksgiving at the ranch. Were they all right?

She worried about David too, out in the storm with Patsy, their border collie, leading the dairy herd back to the barn. She breathed a short prayer for both husband and sister as a sharp crack of lightning sent a tree crashing down somewhere in the nearby mountains and a horrendous peal of thunder rocked the house almost as much as the morning's earthquake had.

"Anything on the radio yet?" David asked as he let the kitchen door slam behind him. When Pam shook her head, he continued, "It looks bad out there. I think it's going to snow tonight. I'm going to take the pickup and go into town for some news."

"I'll go with you." She started for her coat, but David protested.

"It's already pretty cold. I might have to walk back in. And Sandy and Bob might still make it. We did expect them sometime this afternoon, didn't we?"

"But with the earthquake?"

"They're two hundred miles away. They may not even have felt it. You stay here and keep that soup hot, okay? I'll find out where the quake hit and how long the storm is expected to last, and I'll be back before dark. Anything you might need soon from the store?"

She wrote out a short list of staples and supplies. "Now be careful," she called as he dashed to the truck. "Turn around and come back if the road's bad, and spend the night in town if the storm gets worse."

After the blue pickup truck disappeared beyond the trees, Pam knelt by the slipper chair near the stove. She let the ready tears fill her eyes and wet her soft, round face as she prayed again for all her loved ones' safety.

"Dear, dear Lord, please be good to Sandy. She's spent half her life taking care of Mother while she was sick, and then raising me. She put Bob through dental school. Now, at last, things are easy for her. Please, oh please, don't let her be hurt."

The storm seemed to be easing a little, and she busied herself straining the morning's milk into its silvery cans. Their herd was too small to be commercially profitable. David was always saying it was really too small to call a "herd." They used some of the milk from the half dozen cows themselves, sold a little to a few neighbors, and made butter and cheese to sell to a few restaurants in town.

Pam knew David would be gone for two or three hours, but her ears caught each new sound as she listened for the pickup to lumber up the drive. He was back sooner than she had dared hope. Patsy, of course, heard him first and ran, tail whipping, to the door. Pam followed the dog. She gasped as she saw David's pale lips and stricken eyes. "David, what's happened?"

He slumped into a kitchen chair. "I gather our radio still isn't working?"

"No, it isn't. The news is bad, isn't it? The quake hit the city hard, didn't it?"

He shook his head and little rivulets dribbled from his rain-soaked, straw-colored hair, trickling down his ruddy cheeks and dripping from the blunt end of his nose. He drummed the table with his sturdy fingers.

"David, what happened?"

Pam slipped into the chair opposite as he began to speak haltingly. "No one in town really knows what happened either, Pam, but there are some terrible rumors. Jack Turner, at the TV store, has a satellite receiver, you know, and he's gotten some stations inland—Sacramento, I guess."

"Sacramento! Nothing closer than that?"

"No. And that's not the half of it, Pam. There seem to have been major earthquakes all over the world. Communications are a mess everywhere. Ham operators are practically the only source of information all up and down the West Coast."

"The City? Or San Jose?"

"San Francisco apparently didn't have any more than its share of quake damage, but there was a tsunami, a tidal wave. I'm sure it's an exaggeration, Pam, but they're saying the lowlands are devastated. I didn't hear anything about San Jose. There's just no way to get any specific information. Maybe in a few days."

Pam shivered as he continued. "But it's all over the world. China, Japan, Italy, Russia even. In fact, there's practically no news out of Russia."

"But that's not earthquake country, not most of Russia anyhow. I guess the southern part, but—"

"There's no official word from Moscow, but meteorologists in Germany are reporting sudden and terrible storms all over Eastern Europe."

"Like here? David, what's happening?"

"That's what everyone wants to know. Between the earthquakes and the hail and electrical storms, we just don't know. There's something else, though."

He looked down at the waxed wood tabletop, then up at Pam. "It all seems to be centered in Israel. The worst of the earthquakes seems to have happened right around Jerusalem. Apparently that military buildup we've been hearing about in Syria and Iraq was more than a show of force to support the Arab bloc raids. The Russians moved a lot of troops across Jordan last night."

Pam gasped. "War? Nuclear war?"

"No, not so far as I can find out. This Sacramento station suggested some nuclear weapons may have exploded, but probably by accident. At least there has been no retaliation, not by men anyhow."

"Thank God for that. But, David, think of what you're saying. An army invading Israel, a tremendous earthquake there, earthquakes and terrible storms all over the world. David, that's—"

"Armageddon?" The word dropped with an almost audible thud and lay between them in the silence. "Of course it isn't." David picked up the almost unspeakable thought. "It isn't, because the Lord hasn't come yet for the church, and the Beast hasn't been revealed, and all the other signs haven't come. But it is so close. I ran into Pastor Frank in town, and we both said 'Ezekiel 38 and 39' in almost the same breath."

"'Lift up your head, your redemption draweth nigh,'" Pam quoted. "The hymn makes it sound so glorious. But, David, I'm frightened. I'm terribly frightened."

"Me too, Pam. We've been told all our lives we were living in the last days. I know the Lord might come anytime. But now? Why now? I don't know what's happening. I know He's in control, but I'm scared too."

Arm in arm they knelt, poured out their fears to God, and prayed for his guidance, as the wind and rain raged outside the isolated ranch house.

2

Helen Just's first conscious thought that same morning was of the asynchronous clanging of her grandfather clock. Her bed seesawed from head to foot, and she dug the heels of her hands and feet into the soft mattress to ride out the pitching. There was a crash from the living room, and the clock stopped chiming.

"Art?" she wailed. "Art, you're not still sleeping, are you?"

"It's just a little earthquake, Helen. Let's not panic." Art rolled heavily in his twin bed and faced his still-trembling wife. He fumbled for the light switch. "Power's off. We can't do much until it gets lighter. Go back to sleep."

"I heard a crash. I think the clock fell over." Helen felt the floor with her bare feet. "I can't find my slippers, Art."

"If the darn clock fell over, it will still be there in

the morning. I'm not going to start prowling around a dark house when there's probably broken glass on the floor. If you want to go trip over something and get yourself cut up, go ahead. What time is it, anyhow?"

"It must be six o'clock or so. It's starting to get light. Art, will you please get up and help me find my slippers?"

"I guess I might as well. I'm not going to get any more sleep anyhow." He pushed himself upright on the edge of the bed, kneeled and stretched an arm under his wife's bed. "Here's one. The other one must be on your side."

"I found it, way up against the wall. How did it get there? You know I always put them right by the night table so I can find them in the dark."

"We did have an earthquake," Art sighed. "I thought you'd noticed." He wrapped his robe around his ample trunk, as Helen slipped into her smart, sleek, pink negligee. "Go check out your precious clock. I guess I can see well enough to check the lesser things, like windows."

Art glanced at the skylight in the cathedral ceiling of the formal dining room, walked across the kitchen, and turned the knob on the garage door. "The cupboard doors are open, but there doesn't seem to be much damage out here," he called. "Hey, what's the matter? I can't get the door open."

Helen screamed. "Oh, Art, come quick. It's terrible. Oh, Art! The clock! My porcelains! The pictures! Oh, Art, the children's pictures all fell off the mantle."

"I'll be there in a minute, dear. Something's wrong with the garage door." He pulled the knob slightly upward, and the jammed door flipped toward him. "I think we've got a real problem. Something's settled. The door frame's twisted a little."

He walked out into the garage, which was lighted by dawn from its east window. "Oh, no!" He picked up the heavy wrench, which had fallen from its hook, and stared at the bare, dented metal in the middle of the hood of his gold Buick. After a brief look he determined he had found the worst of the damage, and he returned to Helen. She was standing beside the mantle, her long, carefully manicured fingers buried in her short, blue-gray curls.

"Oh, Art," she sobbed. "Everything's such a mess. It will take days to pick it up. And the clock."

Art's eyes followed her gesture to the tall, cherry clock case, face down on the floor. Shards of broken glass formed a halo around its arched top. "I'm sure it can be fixed, Helen," he soothed, muttering "unfortunately" under his breath. "I wonder if the car insurance covers earthquake damage."

"The car insurance? What happened to the car?"

"A monkey wrench fell on it."

"Oh," she shrugged. "Is that all?"

"Wait until you see it. There's a mighty ugly dent in the hood."

Helen knelt and said, "Look at the pictures, the way they stacked up here at the end of the fireplace."

"Looks like they just waited in line and slipped off the end of the mantle one at a time, doesn't it?" Art wanted to smile at the image, but Helen was whining again as she turned each, large, framed photograph face up and looked at the loved faces torn by the broken glass.

Their son, Paul, looked so handsome in his Marine Corps dress blues. That picture had been taken just a few weeks ago, before he left to join the United Nations Peacekeeping Force in the Sinai. And Paul's kid sister, Terry, in her wedding dress, looked up at her husband, Jim. Little Jimmy, Jr., cunning in cap and gown for his kindergarten graduation, shared a double, gilt frame with a picture of his baby sister, Tammy.

"Go call Jim's parents," Helen said, remembering that the grandchildren were in San Mateo with their other grandparents while Jim and Terry enjoyed a second honeymoon in Hawaii. Then Helen remembered that Paul, too, was in danger, from the threatened Russian invasion of Israel. She switched on the television set, but the power was still off.

Art came back in as she was staring at the dark screen. "Phone isn't working. The long-distance lines are probably all tied up. I tried the portable radio in the kitchen, but I can't get anything but static. Helen, I think this may be the Big One . . . the one we've all been worried about for years. I think I'll take a walk downtown and see how the rest of the town fared. Maybe somebody's been able to get a call through or pick up some news from a more powerful radio."

"Don't be long, Art. Hurry back as soon as you find out anything." Her strident whining had softened now. "Please."

A few blocks away, Pastor Frank Thomsen had wakened to the jolting too. He had instinctively flung a long arm across the bed to shelter his wife Anne . . . a wife who wasn't there.

It had been nearly three months since Anne had gone to be with the Lord. Her death had been so sudden. Women of barely forty weren't supposed to have strokes. The shock of again finding her place in the bed empty startled him more than the earthquake.

He waited a few moments until the tremors had ceased and the rattling of his bedroom windows had quieted. He breathed a silent prayer for "those of your people who are in danger, Lord," and turned on the bedside radio. Like his parishioners, he found the power off. The transistor radio in the kitchen crackled softly and died when he tried it. It was Anne who had always kept fresh batteries in it, he remembered.

The refrigerator had opened, and a few bottles had fallen from the shelves. Frank reached for a handful of paper towels and stooped to scoop up catsup, mustard, sweet pickles, and broken glass from the floor.

I'll mop it up later, he thought as he returned to the lonely bedroom to dress. Then, finding no more serious damage and noting no obvious distress from his neighbors' homes, he went into his study. As Frank picked up his Bible, his eyes fell on his sermon notes for next Sunday. He planned to begin a series on the book of Job.

About an hour later, fortified as always by the quiet time with his God, Pastor Thomsen slipped on his jacket and stepped outside. Noting a familiar portly figure ambling down the block, he called, "Art? Everything all right at your place?"

"Hello, Frank. Yeah, we have a little broken glass. Helen's precious grandfather clock fell over, and a wrench fell on my car and gave it a nasty dent, but there's nothing really serious. How about you?"

"Some stuff fell out of the refrigerator and made a mess on the kitchen floor. But I thought I'd better go up and look the church over. Want to walk along?"

"Sure. Might as well." Art panted a bit as he hustled to keep pace with his pastor's long, purposeful stride. "Helen is pretty upset, and I, well, I just needed to get out for a few minutes. You haven't gotten any news, have you? We're a little worried about the grandkids in San Mateo. This was bad enough here. It could have been real serious down there."

"No. I tried the radio but the power's off, and I guess the batteries are dead in the portable."

"I told Helen I'd go downtown and see if I could find anyone who knew anything."

"Good idea." Frank slipped his key in the lock on the church office. "I'll go along with you after we take a quick look around here."

The two men were in the church no more than ten or fifteen minutes. Frank shivered as they left. "Guess I should have put on a warmer coat."

"Look at those thunderheads." Art shook his head and pointed to the ridge, west of town. "Looks like we're in for a real winter storm on top of the quake. I guess this is going to be a Thanksgiving to remember."

They walked briskly into the sudden wind. Business owners were beginning to drift down to survey damage and clean up debris. They shouted greetings against the gathering storm, sympathizing with one another's losses, assuring each other that it could have been much worse, and asking the inevitable, "Have you had any word from the City?"

A knot of neighbors had collected around Jack Turner's TV shop. "Bet Jack's got a generator going and is getting something from his satellite dish," Art said, as he and Frank quickened their pace and joined the eager group.

As they edged through the crowd, they heard garbled snatches of rumors from panicked voices nearly as uninformed as themselves: "had something from the City for a few minutes, and then, whoosh, it just stopped" . . . "tidal wave" . . . "all over the world: Israel, Russia, Australia—"

"Hey, Tom. Tom Braden, what's the news?" Frank called to one of the church elders, who stood fairly near Jack Turner's operating television set. Tom obviously had no intention of moving from his listening post, but he waved as the two pushed closer to him.

"Hi, Art. Gosh, Pastor Frank, it sounds to me like the end of the world."

"Was it bad in the City, Tom?"

"In the City! Pastor, they were broadcasting from there, reporting on the earthquake damage, and then they started warning everyone to evacuate all the low places because there was a tidal wave coming. And then they just quit broadcasting. They just stopped!"

"Maybe they lost their power supply, Tom," Frank said. But Tom shook his head and continued.

"We got a station from inland someplace . . . Sacramento, I think. They had a guy up in a plane, and he said it's gone."

"What do you mean? What's gone, Tom?" Art pleaded, seriously concerned now for his grandchildren.

"San Francisco! Well, not all of it, I guess, but all but the tops of the hills. He said this huge wave rushed in, and when it went out there were no buildings left except on top of the hills."

Punctuating Tom's words, the hills west of town suddenly lit up with great streaks of lightning and echoed with peals of thunder. Rain began to fall in huge, cold, harsh drops, as another voice from the crowd picked up the terrible story.

"That's not the half of it. There have been earthquakes and tidal waves all over the world. They say the worst quake of all was over in the Middle East, in Israel. That whole army just about got wiped out by landslides and sinkholes."

Art thought of his son Paul. "The Russian Army?" he asked, hoping it wasn't the U.S. Marines' peacekeeping force that had been hit.

"Yeah. I guess we don't have to worry about the 'Ruskies' anymore. They started to roll into Israel, you know, from Syria and Iraq, and all heck broke loose," said the man in the crowd.

"The situation sounded bad on the news last night, but the Ruskies hadn't started to move yet," said Art.

"No, Art, but those countries are so small," Frank said as he shook his head sadly. "If Russia started a mass movement, its army could be across the Israeli borders in just a few hours."

"They started to move last night—dawn, their time. It was on the eleven o'clock news. The United

Nations was trying to get them to stop. But I guess it
didn't work, because they did invade. And everybody
figured the Israelis would just have to give in, because
they knew the President wouldn't dare send our boys
in, and nobody else is strong enough." Jack had to
pause for breath. "And then, just as the shelling started
in Jerusalem, this earthquake came, and that was the
end of that."

"See, Pastor," Tom interrupted. "Just like the end
of the world."

The rain was turning to hail now, and the wind
chilled Pastor Thomsen's lean body as the news chilled
his heart. There was a piece missing in the jigsaw
puzzle that formed in his mind. "Is there any news out
of Russia itself?" he asked.

"Now that you mention it, I haven't heard any,"
Tom answered. "But there are reports of damage from
so many places, maybe Russia just hasn't made the
news yet."

Another voice from the crowd broke in. "No. The
announcer mentioned a few minutes ago that there are
reports from almost everyplace else besides Russia.
Where there haven't been earthquakes, there've been
reports of awful storms." The man looked toward the
western sky and pulled his collar up around his neck.
"Lightning, thunder, and hail. But he also said they
couldn't get any radio communication from anyplace at
all in Russia, or any of those places that *used* to be
Russia."

"I'd better get home to Helen. She'll be frantic.
Not that I have much comfort to offer, but at least I

should be with her. You're still welcome for dinner tomorrow, Frank," Art added.

"I think I'll skip it, Art. My apologies to Helen, but I think I have a new sermon to prepare for Sunday."

Art turned away from the crowd. Just then, David Cristman approached and hailed his pastor. "Frank, Frank, have you heard any news?"

"David, good to see you. How are things at the ranch?"

"Pretty good. We didn't have much quake damage, but the power's off. I guess that's true here too. But somebody said Jack had a generator going and a TV on."

"Yes. It's bad, David, bad all over."

"I've got to head home soon. Pam's alone, and this storm's going to close the roads before long. But Pam's worried about her sister Sandy and brother-in-law in this quake; they were coming from San Jose for Thanksgiving. The Middle East situation was desperate when we went to bed last night too."

Frank slumped, and his worried gray eyes met David's questioning blue ones. Frank repeated the frantic reports he had just heard. He was surprised when the younger man suddenly whispered the words he, himself, had been unwilling to voice.

"It fits, doesn't it? Precisely and perfectly. It's the battle of Ezekiel 38 and 39."

"Well, Tom said it was the end of the world, David. But I don't think it's the end. And I hope I know better than to try to force God's Word to fit the circumstances. But, yes, I think it's the beginning of the end. Look up, David. He's coming soon."

David Cristman headed home to Pam, and Frank Thomsen went back to his study. Pushing aside the notes on Job, Frank turned quickly to the text he had decided to use on Sunday. Then he folded his hands on his desk and bowed his head, praying for the injured and the frightened all over the world.

Soon his lips stopped moving, and he rested his head on his hands, listening. After a long silence, he lifted his head and reached again for the discarded note pad. Perhaps it was a good time to start a series on Job after all.

3

Ahundred miles south, on a secluded beach, Bob and Sandy Peters' motor home swayed dizzily, tipped about thirty degrees seaward, and righted itself with a jolt.

Ten-year-old Mark bounced from the over-cab bunk and landed in an awkward sprawl on the sofa bed occupied by his parents. "Ouch!"

Bob was wide-awake in an instant. "Are you all right, Son?"

"Yeah, Dad. I think I twisted my knee when I fell. That's all. Boy, that was some shake."

Jonathan climbed down from the bunk as Sandy examined Mark's knee. At twelve, Jonathan was much too grown up to show fear over a mere earthquake. "It just seems worse in the camper. We'd probably have slept right through it if we'd been home."

Sandy grinned as Mark stood and gingerly tested his knee, which didn't seem seriously injured. "I knew there was a good reason why I didn't want you guys to drag me to a camp-out on the way to Pam and David's."

"Well, we're all wide-awake now, so let's see if we can find a few mussels to take on up with us. Come on, kids, get your old clothes on." Bob found his glasses, pulled on a pair of jeans, and hustled outside; but Sandy noticed he stopped to check over the motor home while he waited for the boys to join him. "The propane tanks look fine, Sandy, but you'd better take a look inside before you start breakfast."

Mark and Jonathan dashed for the nearest tide pools, where Bob soon joined them in the hunt for mussels. With so little competition in the November chill, they quickly filled their bucket and returned to the motor home where Sandy forked hot French toast onto their plates.

"I think I'll just stack the dishes and wash them when we get to the ranch," she remarked as Bob hustled the boys to the nearby restrooms.

"Shush," he gasped suddenly. "What was that noise?" He looked out the window, then yelled after his sons. "Get back here, now! Now!"

Sandy looked out then, and turned, puzzled, to her husband. "What happened? It looks like the tide just went out, but I've never seen it go so fast."

"I'll explain later. Just get everything ready to roll the minute the boys get back." Bob jumped into the driver's seat and started the engine. "Hurry!" he called to the boys, who were on their way back to the motor home.

The door slammed shut behind them, and Bob

seemed not to hear their protests as he gunned the motor and wheeled the motor home onto the paved lane. "Get off the beach, quick," he called to a man standing outside a tent. Passing the only other camper, he called out again, "Make for high ground."

"Go, baby, go," he muttered as they began the steep climb from the beach to the Coast Highway high above. He didn't speak until the motor home was gliding smoothly up the gently curving, cliff-hugging road. "Tsunami."

Sandy looked back, down to the beach they had fled. "It's gone! Bob, the beach is gone. The surf is right under us."

The other motor home bobbed like a rubber ball in a whirlpool. If there were still people in it, they would be screaming for help; but the screams could never be heard above the roar of the tidal wave. And it wouldn't matter if they could be heard. There was no way to help them.

Sandy reached out and hugged Mark and Jonathan close to her. "Bob, how did you know?"

"I guess I must have read it somewhere. I'm not sure. All I know is that when I realized the tide had gone out with that sudden whoosh, something or someone, told me to get out of there."

"Thank God," Sandy breathed, as she looked to each of the three men she loved.

"Thank God," Bob echoed. "There may be another wave." He turned up a narrow, rural road. "If I remember right, this is a fairly good road, and it climbs fast."

"Should we try to get home, Bob? We'll probably

have some damage. My sister will understand if we don't show up."

"I don't know. It depends on where the quake was centered. We may not have that much damage. On the other hand, we may not have a house." Bob fiddled with the radio dial, but was rewarded only with static.

"Does that mean the stations in the City are all off the air, Dad? That sure would be bad news."

"Oh, no, Jonathan. I'm sure it isn't that bad. We'll get something when we get out of these hills." Bob's voice reassured everyone but himself.

Bob maneuvered the motor home down the steep eastern slope of the first ridge, past scattered vacation cabins and second-growth redwood groves. "We'll pick up a Santa Rosa station when we get down to the river."

As they dropped over the last steep ridge, Sandy tried to stifle a gasp. "Oh, Bob, what's happened?" Below, the river wound through its gravel bed, and River Road wound beside it. But the once-idyllic beach was strewn with debris. "Bob, the fishing camp! There was a store here, and cabins."

"Could the wave have come this far up the river, Dad?"

Bob shook his head slowly. "It's hard to believe, Jonathan, but it must have."

"Shouldn't we stop, Bob? Someone may be trapped in the wreckage."

Bob turned onto River Road. "We don't dare, Sandy," he sighed. "The next wave may get this far too. Besides, it doesn't look like anyone could possibly have survived."

The road itself was still wet. Mud floes crossed it in several places, and Bob found it difficult to maneuver the big motor home around first a mud slide on the north side, then a washout on the south. Other cars joined them, pulling out from rocky lanes into the slowly moving chain that was the only way out of the rugged but populous resort area.

Bob fiddled with the radio again, scanning the dial as they edged east toward the freeway. A voice spoke out from an unfamiliar setting on the dial and they listened in open-mouthed shock.

". . . San Francisco, wiping out most of the city, except for the hilltops. The waves have gone back now, taking most of the Sea Cliff, Outer Richmond, and Sunset districts with them. The Bay has risen into the South of Market and Financial districts, but many of the newer, earthquake-resistant high rises there appear to still be standing. Our sister station reports that it can probably be back on the air within a few hours, from its Embarcadero Center studios."

As they approached the freeway they could see it was already jammed. Bob turned up a frontage road. "Most of these people have no idea where they are going. If we take back roads where we can, we'll make a lot better time, and probably save gas too."

"Are we low on gas? I thought you filled up yesterday."

"I did, but if we have to crawl through a traffic jam, we'll eat it up fast. And it may be hard to get more."

THE REVELATION

The voice on the radio faded out, and Sandy reached over to tune it in again as Bob concentrated on driving along the country roads.

"What about the South Bay?" Sandy muttered anxiously. She wasn't sure she really wanted to hear what had happened in the Santa Clara Valley.

As if he had heard her question, the radio announcer broke through the static: "We have a late report from San Jose, stating that the South Bay area has had substantial earthquake damage. There is extensive flooding in lowland areas such as Milpitas, and disaster crews are fighting numerous fires caused by downed power lines and gas leaks. The most critical situation there, though, is the collapse of Anderson Dam, which sent a torrent of water rushing through Morgan Hill and southeast San Jose."

Bob bit his lip as Sandy cried out, and Jonathan found his horror mirrored in Mark's eyes, as each envisioned their beautiful new split-level home, which was nestled into a hillside just below the Anderson spillway. How many times they had joked, as they planted groundcover on the slope, that they'd sure be in trouble if the dam ever broke.

"I guess we head for the ranch," Bob said flatly, as the radio voice continued its litany of tragedy.

"And now to the network for a worldwide wrap-up."

The voice that followed was tired. One didn't need television to see a drawn mouth, sagging eyelids, and dropped chin or to hear the drone of words and numbers beyond comprehension.

"For those of you who have just managed to tune

in, here's a brief recap of the disasters that have struck our world in the last several hours. Late last evening, our time, the previously reported Russian and Arab troop masses suddenly moved from their positions in Syria and Iraq into Israel, as had been feared. An ultimatum was issued by the Arab bloc forces, and the Knesset continued to meet in secret, round-the-clock session. In a special session of the General Assembly, the United Nations voted to censure Russia and the Arab nations, which had invaded Israel over the past several days. The Secretary General, Lucio Crosetti, was directed to exert the full authority of his office to negotiate a truce."

Bob snorted. "What full authority of his office?"

The announcer droned on. "The invasion and the truce seem to be moot points now, in light of fragmented reports coming out of the Middle East. There, an earthquake of unprecedented violence has disrupted all travel. Much of the invading force has been destroyed by landslides. The rest of the region is in total disarray, as landmarks have been obliterated and roads have disappeared under slides or into gaping cracks in the earth."

"Ezekiel 38 and 39?" Sandy murmured.

"There's a resemblance, but we're not quite ready for Armageddon."

"I've read that some Bible experts think the battle in Ezekiel is a different one, earlier, Bob."

"Self-styled experts say a lot of things, but the Word is perfectly clear. The Rapture, the Beast, Armageddon, and the establishment of the Kingdom. We have to be careful not to let events confuse us."

THE REVELATION

I wish I were so sure, Sandy thought, *but I just don't feel as certain about the end-time prophecies as he is.* She spoke softly. "I wish my faith were as strong as yours, Bob. But I am sure of one thing——there are a lot of people in need of our prayers right now."

Though Sandy's eyes were as dark and wide as her sister Pam's, her tears came much less easily. Still, her long lashes were wet as she bowed her head. Her sons each took one of her clammy, trembling hands as she asked God for mercy and strength.

Bob drove on through the golden hills, searching out back roads familiar from his childhood. Dark thunderheads formed above the western ridge. "Just what we need," he muttered. "A storm."

The valley narrowed at Cloverdale, and there were no more back roads. The Peters' motor home joined the congealed mass of cars, trucks, and recreational vehicles clawing their way slowly up the Redwood Highway. Bob turned the radio on again; but the station, from Sacramento, came in only intermittently.

He caught fragments of news——ferocious electrical storms and giant hailstones all over the globe, but wreaking special havoc on Russia and eastern Europe. Earthquakes in Australia, in the Mediterranean, Japan, China, the Ohio Valley, as well as the one California had just experienced. Volcanic eruptions in Latin America, Alaska, Iceland. Ash was spreading quickly and thickly over the populated portions of both hemispheres, causing darkness at midday in such scattered cities as Buenos Aires, London, and Vancouver.

It was only a little past noon in Mendocino County as the Peters crossed the county line, but it was growing dark there, too, because of the storm. Already they were being pummeled by bitter winds and hailstones.

"Do we have the tire chains, Bob?" Sandy asked.

"Chains? It's only Thanksgiving. It never snows this early here."

"Lots of things are happening today that never happen," Jonathan interrupted.

"True, Son. Yes, Sandy, the chains are in the back storage compartment, but I don't really think we'll need them."

The creeping line of vehicles seemed to carry them along like a staggering conveyor belt. It was after three o'clock when they turned off the highway to drive the last few miles up to the Cristman's ranch. Half an hour later, still short of their goal, they drove up past the snow level, and Bob and Jonathan had to get out and put on the tire chains.

It was after four o'clock, and dark as midnight, when Pam heard the labored lumbering of the motor home. "It's Sandy and Bob, David. They've made it!"

Pastor Thomsen moved slowly toward the pulpit of the soaring redwood A-frame chapel. From filled pews and extra rows of folding chairs, faces looked past him. Eyes strained but could not see the redwood grove beyond. The view was crazed, distorted. A maze of cracks marred the shattered window that had been the church's most beautiful feature.

Frank Thomsen's melancholy deepened as he looked out at the faces—some familiar, some strange. They had come here for reassurance, for hope in a world that seemed, literally, to be falling apart. *God help me,* he prayed silently. *Give me words of consolation for these, Thy beloved.*

As he began to speak, Frank realized his message would be a surprise to most of his listeners. Tom Braden was expecting a rousing prophetic exposition. Art Just wanted to know why his faithful Christian family had been caught up in God's righteous judgment. Helen needed to be reminded that she would be reunited with her children in heaven. The Peters begged for encouragement to pick up the pieces and start over. And the Cristmans sought ways to help.

"I had planned to begin a series of sermons from the book of Job today. After the events of last Wednesday, noticing as did many of you the similarity of those events to certain prophetic passages, I changed my plans. But the Lord changed them back. I do not know the times and the seasons." Frank sighed as he reached for his Bible. "I do not know when the Lord will return, physically, though I most assuredly know he will. But I do know that he is in control. Shall we turn to Job, chapter 1, verse 21."

He opened his Bible and read the text he had chosen the afternoon of the earthquake. "'The LORD gave, and the LORD has taken away; Blessed be the name of the LORD.'"

"I know," he continued gently, "how much the Lord has taken from some of you this week. I see Bob and Sandy Peters, frequent visitors here, who have learned that their home and virtually all their possessions were swept away when the Anderson Dam broke near San Jose. Bob, Sandy, I know you can bless the name of the Lord, because you and your sons are with us today due to a series of coincidences that were not really coincidences."

He looked at the Justs and knew that Helen had not slept for three nights. "We do share your grief, Art and Helen. We have listened with you to the news that the beachfront hotels on Waikiki were swept aside like toy buildings, leaving few survivors. We know you have not heard if your daughter and her husband were among those few. We know, too, that you have had news about your son, and that that news is tragic. It will take time, but you will learn to bless the name of the Lord for sparing your grandchildren, and for the assurance that your children were his children too.

"I am certain there is no one here today without a grief, a pain, a need. And so I am going to ask you to join hands, each with the brother or sister next to you, as we call upon the Lord of Creation for his mercy and his healing."

After the sermon on Job, Frank concluded his benediction. Then, as the congregation stood and gathered its belongings, he spoke once more. "Could I have your attention for just a minute? I have a note here from David Cristman. But instead of my reading it, I'll let David give you his message himself. David?"

As most of the people in the church craned their necks to see the speaker, David waved a hand above the crowd. "I'm over here," he called. "Our power's still out at the ranch. We slaughtered a calf a couple of weeks ago, so we've got a load of thawed beef in our pickup in the parking lot. If any of you have no plans for dinner, we've got a lot of meat to use up, so we're going to have a barbecue in about an hour."

Neighbors shouted offers of help, while strangers murmured shy questions. "Everybody's invited," David continued. "If you've got something at home to bring over and put on the table, fine. If you're stranded in town because of the quake, come and be our guests. See you later."

*　　*　　*

Sandy laughed for the first time in three days as she helped Pam turn steaks on borrowed grills. "I think our loaves and fishes are being multiplied, unless your calf has wings. Or isn't that a turkey turning on the Hill rotisserie?"

"And it's a good thing too. I know there weren't this many people in church, but if they need food I'm glad we have it to give," Pam responded. "Some of them probably just needed a place to cook what they had, like us."

"What many of us need most, Pam, is the fellowship," said Frank, smiling as he strolled past the borrowed grills. "I knew it, but I didn't know how to provide it. We're all grateful to you and David."

"But, Frank, we really did need a way to use the meat before it spoiled. We didn't know if the power had come back on in town, but we figured we could use charcoal grills outside if we had to."

At a table across the room, David and Bob were conversing with Jack Turner. "We need some expert advice," David explained. "I've been planning on putting up a windmill out at the ranch, and now it seems fairly urgent. I've got a few books, but—"

"Got just the thing over at the TV shop," said Jack. "It's a packaged kit, and the directions are pretty good too. Be glad to help you hook her up once you get a frame up over the treetops."

"Great! Bob's going to be staying here, for a little while anyhow, and we can get to work right away."

"Well, there's just one little problem," Jack expanded. "This kit'll do the job but it's designed for co-generation, for hooking up with the light company. You can use storage batteries, but you need a slew of them."

"That's what I thought. I'd sure like to have a self-sufficient setup. We could probably get the batteries later, when the world gets more or less back to normal."

"Except that the world isn't going to get back to normal, David," Bob grumbled. "With the Lord coming for us any minute, I really think we should use our time more effectively. Or do you figure the unsaved can use the windmill, too, after we Christians have been raptured?"

"Maybe," David answered. "Or, maybe, the Rapture isn't as imminent as we hope."

"That's what I keep trying to tell Tom, here." Jack wriggled over, leaving space for the folding chair Tom Braden carried. "Might be another false alarm, in which case you could be mighty grateful for your own power supply, David. I'm trying to sell him a windmill," Jack explained as Tom set his plate of barbecued chicken on the table.

"Matter of fact, Tom, I'm already sold. I've always liked that saying that you should live your life as if the Lord were coming today, but plan it as if he weren't coming for a thousand years. How soon can we get the kit and get started, Jack?"

"We can go pick one up at the shop this afternoon if you want. I have a key with me."

"All right, we'll run over right after dinner. Now, Tom, Jack, tell us what you hear on the news. We're still cut off out in the country."

"Well, we won't have to worry about that Russian Confederation for quite a while, it sounds like," said Jack. "They say almost all the missile installations were destroyed by the storms and floods. And they lost a big chunk of their army in Israel."

"How bad is the damage in the Middle East?" Bob asked.

"The Arabs won't be starting any more wars right away, either," Tom said. "I hear whole regiments got swallowed up in landslides. There's going to be a whale of an oil shortage, though, with the ports and refineries wrecked."

"That will affect Europe more than us, of course."

"Yes, David, but we lost some refineries, too, to the earthquake and tidal waves. You've got a couple of horses, haven't you?"

David chuckled. "My hobby may turn into an asset after all. I've got the fanciest pair of carriage horses and the smartest surrey, probably the only surrey, in the county."

"Didn't you say you'd picked up an old hay wagon at an auction too?" Tom asked.

"I'd forgotten all about that! It needs a lot of restoration, but after we get the windmill up, maybe I'll haul it out of the shed and get to work on it." David turned back to the outside news. "Is our government getting disaster relief organized at all yet?"

"Not much," Tom replied. "Washington has been taking a beating, along with most of the East Coast, from a mammoth hurricane. And the middle of the country got flattened by the blizzards and hail." Tom shook his head. "If I didn't know better, didn't know

the Rapture of the church had to come first, I'd swear
the Great Tribulation had started."

"People been saying that for hundreds of years,"
Jack shrugged. "No doubt there's been times this bad
before. What do you think, Pastor?" he asked Frank,
who had just joined them.

"As I said this morning, I'm afraid we all try too
hard to see fulfillment of prophecy in any unusual
happening. It does seem to fit, though, doesn't it?
Jerusalem flattened by a giant earthquake. The super-
powers slapped down. And now Europe's finally getting its act together."

"What do you mean, Frank?" David asked.

"I forgot you people still don't have power for
radio or TV. The common market nations called an
emergency meeting Friday. Since Europe seems to
have gotten off fairly easy, they've already agreed to
tighten their alliance. They want to make sure Russia
doesn't ever become a major force again. Their econo-
mies are all so dependent on ours, as well as on
Middle Eastern oil, that they have no choice but to
close ranks. Sounds like they could be merging almost
completely within weeks if this mood of mutual need
persists."

"Good out of evil," David mused.

"Just good, or the divine plan?" Frank asked of no
one in particular.

"And now the ten-nation confederation of Daniel
and Revelation." Bob's voice carried the authority of
conviction. "We have to preach the gospel, Pastor. We
have very little time left."

"Amen to that, Bob." Tom pounded his paper

plate with his chicken drumstick. "We've got to get out there and save the lost, 'cause the Lord's coming any second."

"I was a bit surprised that you decided to go ahead with the study in Job, Pastor Frank," Bob said. "A reminder to us of God's sovereignty is always appropriate, of course. Sandy and I can certainly appreciate that right now. But don't you agree that this situation is a warning, not to Christians, but to the unsaved?"

"Not entirely, Bob. It is that, of course, and we must always consider evangelization our first priority. But—"

Tom interrupted. "Frank, we know what this means. He's coming! We don't have to be patient, because we don't have to wait anymore. But for the lost, tomorrow will be too late. Jesus will have come, and they'll be left behind."

"You're probably right, Tom. Perhaps my invitation should have been stronger."

David smiled encouragement to his pastor. "Frank, it was clear and powerful. How many people came forward anyhow? Eight or ten, it looked like."

"Not all for salvation, David, though there were two. The others were Christians with special needs."

"Two!" Bob stood, as if to begin preaching on the spot. "Two, out of the dozens, at least, who were there looking for the answer, the only answer!"

"Now, Bob." David gently tugged his brother-in-law back into his chair. "Frank preached the message the Lord gave him, and the Lord moved those he wanted to move. We all know the time is short, but for what time is left we each have to go on living. And for many of us, like Art and Helen, that isn't going to be easy."

In many ways it could have been a typical church potluck. As the men discussed the world events of the week, the women gathered in the church kitchen and shared more immediate domestic problems.

"I set that piece of roast beef aside for the Justs," Pam explained, as a helpful hand reached up for it. "I wish they had stayed, but I guess Helen isn't ready to face so many people."

"I understand a little of how she feels. When I think my boys could have been drowned in their beds if we hadn't left home a day early." Sandy shuddered. "I wonder if I will ever forget that camper tossing in the tsunami just below us. It could just as well have been us."

Pam's hand touched her sister's as her friends murmured sympathy and scattered "praise the Lords."

"Weren't you scared to death out on the ranch by yourself, Pam?" Joan Turner queried. "With no power, and no phone, and no one within hailing distance?"

"Well, I wasn't alone. David was there when the quake hit. And we can get by pretty well without electricity for awhile. The freezer's the biggest problem, obviously. You know, we've got that gorgeous Victorian wood stove in the kitchen, and in this weather it's not that bad a way to cook."

"I dashed right out and bought all the canned goods I could pay for," said Tom Braden's wife, Peggy. "And soap, and toilet paper." Peggy was old enough to remember what was scarce during World War II. "You really miss those things if you can't get them."

"I'm afraid there will be a lot of shortages. I've already got Sandy helping me plant more winter vegetables in cold frames out at the ranch."

Sandy rubbed the small of her back and groaned. "Yes, my kid sister is a real slave driver."

The other women smiled as Sandy, a salt-and-peppered head taller, gave her sister an affectionate hug.

Sandy smiled too, but sobered almost immediately. "There are going to be food shortages and epidemics. There are going to be worse times than we have ever seen. But Bob is sure this is further evidence that the Lord is coming very soon."

"Then why are you planting more stuff?" Peggy asked. "The Rapture's coming any day, absolutely any minute."

"Actually, Bob was wondering about that too, but the Bible does say not to set dates. I believe he's coming soon too, but others have believed that before. Anyhow, if we are taken away, the people left behind are going to be very hungry."

"Well, Tom and I think it's more important to get out and preach the gospel, while there's still time," said Peggy.

Sandy nodded. "And people are confused and frightened now. They are going to recognize their need for God and be more open. I think God brings good from all things, and I think we're going to see a great revival if the Lord does delay his coming."

5

It should have been a somber group. The Little Valley Church had begun Easter Sunday with a service of remembrance for Paul Just, whose body had just been returned from Egypt, and for his sister and brother-in-law, who had died in Hawaii and whose remains had never been found.

But the winter of grieving was over, and even Art and Helen had agreed the theme of the service would be resurrection and joy. So it did not seem inappropriate on this warm spring day for the group to picnic together in the redwood grove after church.

Pam and Sandy, along with the other women, set heaping platters of meat loaf and fried chicken in a line down the center of the longest table. Bubbly casseroles, heaping salad bowls, and thick-sliced loaves of home-baked bread were placed in clusters around the platters. A smaller table held an abundance of apple pies, and Jonathan and Mark Peters churned the old-fashioned ice cream freezers.

The devastation of the previous Thanksgiving was nearly forgotten, as neighbors chatted about the sudden peace and prosperity they were enjoying.

"It's hard to realize it's been less than six months," Sandy reflected. "I thought we'd lost everything when I heard that the dam had broken and our home was destroyed. But Bob and I are so happy here. Little Valley really needed another dentist, especially with all our fellow 'refugees.' Bob has more patients than he can handle. We're starting work this week on our new house on a corner of Pam and David's ranch."

Helen's face had aged, and she still seldom smiled. But the sadness did retreat as she glanced at the group of children playing kickball in the parking lot. "It still hurts to realize that Paul and Terry are both gone, but it helps having Terry's children with us. Art and I both love them so. Life does go on, and we know we will all be together again one day."

Pam laid her hand gently on the older woman's arm. "Praise the Lord. It hurts me so to think of the millions who don't have that comfort, Helen. They can only feel the pain and ask why."

"But so many have turned to the Lord," Sandy reminded them.

Jonathan interrupted to offer his mother a spoonful of ice-creamy goodness. "Is it ready yet, Mom?"

"Not quite," she grinned. "Keep turning a little longer." She turned back to Pam and Helen, and to her previous comment. "I've never heard of the gospel spreading so fast, or being so widely accepted. Have you?"

"Not since the book of Acts," Pam answered. "Just look around you. Half of these people have come to the Lord since the earthquake."

"When do we eat, ladies?" Frank inquired.

"Just as soon as you blow your whistle and ask the blessing, Pastor."

David and Art discussed the latest news as they moved from the laden serving table to the smaller table at which their wives were seated with Bob and Sandy. "I still think it was God's righteous judgment on those godless Ruskies and his way of getting the world back to the Word."

"You're right, up to a point, Art. Obviously God was in the bad times, and obviously we're seeing a revival now. But I still think this peace is very temporary."

"David, we've got a strong, democratic system of government established almost worldwide, for the first time in history. With Russia flat and China too busy trying to feed herself to think about war, we've got a secure peace. The UN finally has enough power to put down these petty dictators who insist on popping up in all these little countries, and God-fearing men finally have a chance to put God's law into effect."

"I wonder, though," Pam inserted, "if men, God-fearing or not, will ever be able to establish God's law."

"Oh, not permanently, I guess. I know there will be wars again before the Lord comes, but—"

"But you think he won't come for a long time."

Bob refused to share Art's complacency. "Five months ago, Art, you thought the same as we did, that he was coming any minute. Now the UN, under Secretary General Crosetti, has established a sort of *pax Romana,* and you assume, because you want to, that it will last at least for our lifetimes."

Bob laid his fork aside and continued. "I'm absolutely convinced that this new, strong United Nations, which obviously is dominated by Western Europe, is really the ten-nation confederacy."

David gave his brother-in-law a warning glance, but Bob went on anyway. "You know, they've made a firm commitment to support Israel should the Arabs try to attack her again. Crosetti's even given his word that the Jews can build a new temple on the ruins of the Dome of the Rock. It's absolutely amazing. It's the covenant of Daniel, exactly. I don't know what more you're looking for. And there are just ten countries in the Security Council now."

"But, Bob," Art argued, "that covenant was to be between the Jews and the Antichrist. Surely you don't think Crosetti is the Beast."

"He's Italian, 'the Prince of the people that are to come.' He's the leader of a ten-nation confederation. He talks peace. He's certainly got charisma. Why couldn't he be the Antichrist?"

"Oh, Bob," Helen countered. "That's ridiculous. Crosetti is a humble man. He's even given God the glory for his own work as a diplomat. You all heard his speech last week. You heard him praise God for the good weather we've had and for the spirit of cooperation during the rebuilding."

"And for the revival," Pam reluctantly agreed. "He has encouraged the preaching. It isn't likely the Antichrist would do that, is it?"

Bob poked a warning finger at her. "The Antichrist will be the best con man of all time, Pam."

"So you think you have all the answers," Art muttered. "Times have been tough before, and Christians have been sure his coming was just around the corner."

"Read your Bible, Art." Bob's voice had a sharp edge.

David rushed to head off the quarrel. "We all read our Bibles, Bob, but we don't all interpret it the same way. Why should we assume, after all these centuries, that ours is the chosen generation? And does it really matter, as long as we all trust the Lord?"

Bob was not ready to yield. "If you're so sure things are back to normal, or better than normal, Art, what do you think of that astronomer in China?"

"Oh, him. He's nuts. All of the western experts agree that comet will miss the earth by millions of miles. We're in no danger."

"That's what the newspapers say. That's what our good, strong government wants us to think. But I'm not so sure."

Helen looked up. "What comet, Bob? I don't read the papers much, and I'm usually fixing dinner when the TV news comes on." She turned to her husband. "Art, you didn't say anything about a comet."

"I knew you'd worry about it." Art's voice was unnecessarily harsh. "Some Chinese crackpot says there is a new one and it's headed toward us. But as I reminded Bob, the Western experts all agree there is no danger."

Bob opened his mouth to respond, but Sandy cut him off gently. "Would you get me a dish of that ice cream, Bob, before it's all gone?"

Tom was helping Jonathan open the second freezer when Bob strode up. "Seconds already, Bob?" Tom chuckled.

"Not me, Tom. Sandy sent me over to get me away from Art."

Tom glanced toward the Cristmans' table. "He's still at it about how everything's going to be fine now that Crosetti's in charge? Sure doesn't take some people long to forget, does it?"

"You know, Tom, I just can't understand it. Even David acts like the earthquake didn't mean anything at all. Just roll up our sleeves and go back to business as usual."

"And you know something, Bob?" Tom edged away from the crowded picnic tables. "I think Pastor Frank's not much better. If he'd just preach some good old-fashioned expository sermons on prophecy, about how all that's happening fits right into the book of Revelation, these folks would see the light and quit wasting time rebuilding." He glared at Bob. "Why, you're building a new house yourself."

Bob shrugged. "Not that I expect to live in it, but, well, we are a little crowded living with Pam and David. And David did sort of push the site on me."

"David! Now there's the perfect example. As if David doesn't know very well that the Rapture isn't that far—" Tom held up thumb and forefinger. "Not that far away. Why, with his windmill and crops and all, you'd think he was getting ready for the Tribulation, instead of for the Rapture."

"Maybe he is."

"Bob, you don't mean that. David Cristman knows the Scriptures as well as I do," Tom said.

"You mean he should. So should the pastor, and more so. But you just listen to what the pastor says. Sometimes he sounds so vague I wonder if he knows what he believes."

"I did think he'd say something about that comet this morning, Bob. It's right there in Revelation 8. But all we get is 'Though He slay me, yet will I trust Him.' Well, Bob, I trust Him all right, but I know what's coming, and it's about time our pastor made that clear to the rest of these people."

Bob shifted his feet uneasily. "I'm new in town, and it really isn't my place to criticize the pastor, Tom, but I agree. We need more warnings to the unsaved and more end-time teaching. Time is too short for all this emphasis on patience."

6

A few nights later, David and Pam, Bob and Sandy stood alone in the open pasture a few hundred feet from the ranch house. "Quite a display, isn't it?" Bob commented.

The night was patent-leather black with shiny pinpoints of twinkling light. Every few moments a new pinpoint appeared, plunged downward through the starry expanse, and disappeared. "I almost wish I'd let the boys stay up to watch," Sandy breathed, as an especially bright streak slashed the horizon.

"There is supposed to be another shower tomorrow night. Maybe, if they want to, they can stay up for it," Bob agreed. "This could be a once-in-a-lifetime experience. I've certainly never seen anything like it."

After about half an hour the meteor shower slackened, and the four went back into the kitchen. "If no one else is any sleepier than I am, how about some hot chocolate?" Pam asked. Sandy set out heavy pottery mugs, and Pam put fresh milk on the stove to warm.

"Now what do you think, David?" Bob asked, as the two men sat down at the kitchen table.

David shrugged. "People who should know insist this is perfectly normal. We're going through the end of a comet's tail, and we're getting a chance to see some brilliant natural fireworks."

"I didn't ask what experts thought," Bob probed, a self-assured smile on his lips. "I asked what you thought."

It was very late, and David was a trifle annoyed with his brother-in-law. "I think I've seen a brilliant display of God's handiwork. I think we are passing through the tail of a comet. And, Bob, I simply don't know whether that comet and this earth are going to collide."

"And you don't care," Bob chided.

"I didn't say I didn't care. Of course I care. If that happens, the world will suffer horribly. But if this comet really is the great star of Revelation 8, I don't expect to suffer through it, nor do I expect Pam and the rest of you to suffer through it, because I expect the Lord to come for us first."

"He's right, Bob," Sandy pleaded. "If the Lord is coming, He will come, and we will be with Him. If the comet is going to hit, it's going to hit. But why do we have to argue about it?"

Pam poured steaming milk into the cocoa Sandy had spooned into their mugs. "Bob," she asked softly, "will you ask the Lord's blessing on our snack?"

Bob couldn't resist the opportunity she had given

him. "Father," he prayed, "we thank you for this snack, and for the assurance that you will protect us from the coming judgment."

As they sipped the hot cocoa, Pam managed to shift the conversation to a less controversial topic. "Let's invite Tom and Peggy Braden out for dinner tomorrow after church, David."

"Fine with me," he said, as Sandy and Bob nodded assent. Pam moved a large roast from freezer to refrigerator to thaw, and then she and David went upstairs to bed.

Pastor Frank's refusal to preach on the topic of end-time prophecy was obvious and clearly deliberate, Tom and Bob agreed the next day after church as they feasted on Pam's juicy pot roast. "I doubt there's another evangelical preacher in the country who persists in preaching from Job, of all things," Tom grumbled.

"I thought he preached a wonderful message today," Pam protested. "What could we need more than to be reminded that the Lord is the Creator and we are his creatures?"

"We know that," Tom said. "We're all Christians. What we need instead is a preacher who will tell the lost that the Lord is coming and that they'd better get saved before he does!"

David protested, in his pastor's defense. "There have been more altar calls and more souls responding in the last few months than in the past ten years. People are being saved."

"Not enough, David," Tom persisted. "You know

what I think? I think Pastor Frank doesn't really believe the Lord is coming."

"Oh, Tom," Peggy protested.

But Bob found himself nodding. "I think you're right. In fact, last Wednesday in Bible study he as much as said so."

It was Pam's turn, then, to interrupt. "He did not! He said we shouldn't try to force prophecy to fit events. That's all. We just shouldn't try to tell God how to fulfill his word. And Frank's right. We shouldn't."

"We're not trying to," Bob defended. "We're just facing the facts. And here we've got people like Art Just running around saying everything's just fine now that God's judged the sinful Russians. We've got Jack Turner saying if the Lord didn't come after last Thanksgiving, maybe he's not coming at all. And we've got a preacher who isn't saying anything." Bob thumped the table with his fork as he concluded. "There's a comet about to hit the earth, and we've got a preacher who admits he doesn't know what the Bible plainly teaches. We are living on the very brink of the Great Tribulation. It's time, now, for the Lord to rapture the church."

"Who should the pastor tell, Bob? The Lord?" asked David.

"David, you surprise me even more than Frank. You've been raised on the Scriptures. You know he, and we, have an obligation to preach salvation to the lost while there is still time."

"And I'm saying Frank has done that, and is doing it."

"Yes." Pam looked lovingly at her husband.

"David's right. And Frank is right too, to remind us of God's sovereignty and mercy just as he has been doing."

Jonathan had been waiting for a pause in the adult conversation. "Mom, can we go outside and play?"

"Sure." Sandy waved, and the boys hurried out. "Now, would the big boys like to play a little too? This was supposed to be a friendly Sunday dinner."

"Sorry we got so serious, ladies," Bob apologized, pushing his chair back from the table. "Tom, want to see how Dave and I are coming on the new house?"

"Yeah, sure," Tom answered. "But you wait," he muttered. "If things don't change pretty soon, the board of elders is going to be talking about a new preacher."

It was nearly dark when the Sunday evening service ended. "You don't really think Tom was right, this afternoon. Would the elders really ask Frank to resign?" Pam asked, as the Cristmans and Peters drove out the winding road to the ranch.

"I don't know, Pam," David answered. "I hope not. Frank's a good man, a sincere man. But there is a feeling that he isn't meeting the needs of the congregation."

"He's not," Bob muttered.

"Now, Bob, I really appreciate his messages on trust and patience. I know you're confident about what's going on, but my faith just isn't that strong. I don't know what's happening, and I need reminding that the Lord is in charge."

"That proves my point, Pam. If he were preaching the prophetic Word as he should be, you would know what's coming. The Lord is coming for his church. We don't need blind faith. God has given us light."

David glanced from the road to Bob. "The problem seems to be that we don't all see the light the same way. You, Tom, me, I guess, expect the Lord to come for the church before there are any more disasters. Art, Jack Turner, others think what's happening now is no different from what's happened before. They do believe the Lord is coming again, Bob. They just don't see the details the same way we do."

"But if Frank Thomsen were doing his job, they would. Dave, if you really want to help your pastor, quit defending him and have a little talk with him."

"I have, Bob."

"Well, I haven't seen any changes."

"Bob, Frank is as concerned as you are about meeting the needs of the church. In fact, he sought me out to talk about it, not the other way around. He's started, several times, to prepare a series of messages about world events in the light of prophecy, just as you are demanding."

"So, when does the series start?"

"It doesn't, not yet anyhow," David responded. "Frank says he's done a lot of praying and a lot of studying, but—"

"But what?" Pam asked, as David hesitated.

"I don't really know if I should talk about it. After all, Frank did take me into his confidence, ask me for help."

"David, I'm not out to get Frank Thomsen. I want to help him too," Bob said.

"Well, Bob, he told me he just can't prove it. He can't prove to himself that this is the time. Sure, some startling things are happening, but—"

"Can't prove it! For Pete's sake, David, what is the man waiting for? The Beast?"

"Didn't the Lord say, himself, that we were to look up when we saw the abomination?" Pam asked. "And aren't there other passages that also indicate the Beast will be revealed before the Rapture?"

"Crosetti," Bob offered. "Crosetti has been revealed, for those of us who know the Scriptures well enough to recognize him."

"I think you're right, Bob. Frank thinks so too, but he says that every time he starts to prepare a sermon on Crosetti, the Lord turns him back to Job."

"How can he be so sure it's the Lord, David?"

"How can you be so sure it isn't, Bob?"

The adults were quiet, then, as the car climbed the driveway, and stopped in front of the ranch house. "There's going to be more shooting stars tonight, Dad," Mark reminded his father as they climbed out of the car. "Mom said Jon and I could stay up and watch if you said so."

"Okay, if you can stay awake that long," Bob agreed. "But it will be very late."

A few hours later, Mark was caught dozing in his chair, but he awoke when his father tried to carry him up to bed. Mark protested loudly that he was wide awake now, so the boys joined their parents and aunt and uncle in the pasture that night.

THE REVELATION

The meteor shower was even more spectacular than the night before. "Wow!" Jonathan exclaimed more than once as a fiery streak blazed across the sky.

But the sharp whistle caught them completely by surprise. They were looking to the west, over the ocean, when Patsy, who had been lying at David's feet, stood and began to whimper. Then the high whine reached their less-sensitive ears too. They had not yet identified it when the ground shook beneath them, and they whirled to see a cloud of luminous dust rise over Little Valley.

When they realized that the tiny spots of light they saw were a dozen small fires burning in the town, Bob ran for his motor home.

"Take my pickup instead," David called. "Since I'm a volunteer fireman, I already have some fire-fighting equipment in it. I'm going to harness up the wagon and drive it down. We may need to bring a lot of people back out here if those fires spread too much."

Pam and Sandy reacted as quickly as the men. "We'll get some coffee and sandwiches ready while you're harnessing the horses. You may all have a long night of fire fighting."

"We're going too," Mark screamed. "We're going with Daddy."

"No, you aren't." Bob spoke more sharply than he had intended, but he continued turning the truck to head toward town.

"But, Mom," Jonathan pleaded as his father disappeared. "Mom, we're old enough to help. Can't we go with Uncle David?"

She wanted to refuse, to keep the boys safe with her; but as she worked in the kitchen with Pam, she reconsidered. "All right, Jon. You may go if Uncle David doesn't mind. But, Mark—"

The younger boy already knew what she was going to say, and she saw the tears well up in his eyes. "I'm sorry, Mark, but they may be gone a long time. We need a man here to help us." Mark's tears vanished.

Pam smiled as her quick-thinking sister thrust a hamper of sandwiches into the boy's arms. "You can start helping by taking that out and putting it in the wagon. Okay?"

Pam, Sandy, and Mark were hypnotized by the horror they viewed from the upstairs window. The night sky was sunset orange, as spot fires dotted the valley to the east. Little Valley would be a checkerboard of smoldering ruins and smoke-stained survival in the morning. A fringe of flame edged upward across the ridge opposite their own, as that hillside's new spring growth was ravaged.

"Please, God, protect us and our loved ones," Pam prayed, as her fingers unconsciously braided rug strips. "Send rain to douse the fires, and protect your children from the flames."

"Thank God we're on the west side of the valley, where it's not so dry," Sandy said, drawing Mark closer to her.

"But we're not that safe, not in this." Pam didn't want to frighten her sister, but she had seen wildfires. "Mark, you go across to your room and be a forest ranger, will you? If you see any fires coming our way, call right away. Sandy, I'm going outside to check the cows and take a look around."

"Sure. I'll keep watch here, unless there's some way I can help you." Sandy's heart was with her husband, somewhere in the blazing town.

"I won't be outside long." Pam was worried about the men too, and her friends down in the valley. "They'll be safe, Sandy. The Lord is with them."

Pam was in the barn when she heard Mark's call. As she ran toward the house she saw the cause for his alarm. A plume of smoke rose from the woods a few hundred yards from the house. As Sandy and Mark ran toward her from the back door, she pointed back to the house. "Get some heavy blankets and soak them. I'll grab shovels and meet you there."

The fire was larger than it had appeared from the house; and they realized that unless it were quickly controlled it could engulf the ranch.

"Mark," Pam shouted, taking charge immediately. "You go back to the house and find all the hoses you can! There are several in the barn and one or two in the garage. Put them all together and connect them to the front tap. They won't reach this far, but I want them ready if the fire gets closer. Okay?"

"Sure, Aunt Pam." The boy tried to hide the quiver of his lip. "Aunt Pam, there'll be enough water to put it out, won't there?"

"We're going to put it out here, with the blankets," she assured him as she and Sandy beat at the flickering underbrush. "But if it should get closer, we've got a good well, and the new windmill will keep the pump going. Now hurry!"

"Thanks for sending him back away from the fire," Sandy gasped as she laid the steaming blanket aside and picked up a shovel.

"That wasn't why I did it. I think we've got this flare-up under control, but there are probably going to be more. We need those hoses ready."

Pam was right. Three more times that night columns of red smoke were spotted, and Pam, Sandy, and Mark rushed to beat out the flames. Only once did the fire reach the edge of the ranch clearing.

Sandy's lithe frame lifted and beat rhythmically as she flung Pam's best comforter down across the creeping enemy. At first Pam kept Mark busy helping her haul the heavy hoses and point out hot spots, but finally she was forced to yield to his pleas.

"Yes, Mark. Get another blanket and help your mother." Pam dragged the hose alone with strength she didn't know her tiny body possessed, deftly directing the stream of water over both Sandy and Mark as they labored close to the flames.

"Get back!" she shouted suddenly, and they retreated as a burning oak limb fell where they had stood. But in an instant both had dashed forward and smothered the crackling branch.

At dawn they sat on the wide porch, exhausted but safe. "Oh, no!" Pam suddenly started. "I forgot all about the milking."

"Is that all?" Sandy sighed and sponged her tingling arms with cool water. "The men will be back soon. Can't they take care of that so we can get some rest?"

"Cows don't like to wait." A smile cracked Pam's smoke-smudged face. "Besides, the men will be as tired as we are."

"I'll help with the milking. Uncle David taught me." Mark stifled an "ouch" as he uncurled from the porch floor.

"No, Mark. You go upstairs to bed. I'll help," Sandy protested. "Pam and I can take care of the cows if the men don't get back soon."

"You can't milk cows, Mom. Anyhow, I'm a man too. You said so last night," he reminded her.

"And you certainly proved it," Pam said. "He does know how to milk, Sandy. Let him help. By then the others will be back, and we'll all have some breakfast and get a good rest."

But when the milking was finished, husbands and son still had not returned. David and Jonathan had driven the nervous horses into pandemonium. Discovering dozens of terrified victims of the molten meteor pellets and the resulting fires, David had deposited Jonathan on the lawn of the town's tiny hospital.

"You can be more help here than anywhere else, I think," he had assured the boy, who had been insisting on helping to fight the fires. "Firefighting is a job for trained personnel."

"You're sure I can be more help here?"

Peggy Braden, the hospital's nursing supervisor, had overheard the conversation. "Jon, we need a strong pair of arms here for lifting hurt people, and a fast pair of legs for errands. We'd appreciate your help."

David, relieved, smiled his thanks as he left his nephew in the relative safety of the makeshift infirmary on the hospital lawn. He tied the horses, still harnessed to the big, clumsy hay wagon, in a sheltered corner and strode up Main Street to a yellow fire truck, which appeared to be Chief Garrison's headquarters.

"Dave! Dave!" David saw the chief's gloved hand waving above the crowd; he was obviously grateful to see the volunteer firefighter. "Over here! Boy, am I glad to see you. I've got a hundred men here who don't know what they're doing. Take a dozen or so over to Bridge Street. We're losing houses over there. Where are your tools?"

"Have you seen my brother-in-law Bob? He brought my truck down with the tools in it. I followed with the hay wagon. I thought we might need it to take people back to the ranch for shelter."

"Haven't seen him, Dave, but there's an awful lot of confusion around here. Well, scrounge some shovels and try to do what you can with garden hoses."

"How's the water pressure?"

"Holding, so far."

It was dawn when David, worn-out and nursing a blistered arm, returned to the hospital lawn. Jonathan spotted him waiting for one of the women to tear a bed sheet to dress his burns. "Uncle David, have you seen my dad? Nobody here knows where he is."

David frowned at the boy's question. "I'm sure he's all right, Jon. We'll check with Chief Garrison as soon as I get a bandage on this arm. Then we'll load up the wagon with some of these people who aren't too badly hurt and need a place to stay, and we'll all head home."

He pretty much trusted Bob to take care of himself; with over a dozen separate fires in town, it was understandable how the two men had missed each other. Still, Little Valley *was* a small town. David couldn't help but wonder why someone hadn't run into Bob, somewhere, and mentioned it to him.

David sent Jonathan back to check with Chief Garrison for news of Bob, then walked across the trampled lawn to the hospital. "Frank! Hello! Who's in charge around here?"

"Dave Cristman, you are a welcome sight! I hope that arm isn't badly hurt."

"Just singed a little, Frank."

"You've had fire at the ranch too, then?"

"Not that I know of. I left the ranch last night when we first noticed the fires here in the valley. But, as far as I've heard, the normal dampness of the west ridge has protected it from the worst. Frank, I brought the old hay wagon down. There are a lot of people here who don't really need hospital care but do need a safe place to recuperate."

Frank nodded as David continued. "I know thirty or forty percent of the houses in town are uninhabitable, so if you'd point out the neediest, I'll load up and take a dozen or so home with me."

"Have you heard about the Turners, Dave?"

"Burned out? They're welcome at our place."

"Worse than that, I'm afraid. Dave, one of the

meteorites landed on their house. Jack . . . Joan's in surgery right now, but Peggy told me it looks bad."

"Oh, God!" it was a prayer torn from David's heart. "Oh, God, not Jack! The children?"

"They were at the other end of the house. They have some cuts and bruises, but mostly they're scared. David, I know three toddlers can be a handful, but if you and Pam could take them in—"

"Of course, Frank. You know we will."

"Yes, I did know you would. But you'd be surprised at some of the people who have opened their homes. What's the old saying about disaster drawing people together?" Frank shook his head as he continued. "But you and Pam have been that way from the beginning. Well, Peggy's sort of been running the show here. She can tell you where the Turner kids are."

"Fine. I'll talk to her and start loading. By the way, Frank, have you seen anything of my brother-in-law?"

"Why, no. Is he in town?"

"He left in my pickup last night while I was harnessing the horses. And nobody seems to have seen him."

"He probably couldn't find you in the confusion and went on home once the fires were controlled."

"Yes, Frank. That must be it. He'll be at the ranch when we get there."

"Oh, David," Peggy interrupted, with a big hug of gratitude for David's willingness to help the Turners' kids. "Those poor little tykes. They're around back. Rachel Stenberg's looking after them. You know the Stenbergs, don't you? They're teachers at the high school."

"I know Joe. He's in the volunteer fire department too. Aren't they expecting a baby pretty soon?"

"In a few weeks. That's why I set her down with the kids. She was out here trying to help with the injured, and I was afraid she'd hurt herself."

"There are so many hurt, Peggy. After I check things at home, Pam and I will come back and see what we can do here. Tell me who else needs a place to recuperate, and I'll load up the wagon."

Peggy thought a moment. "If you really have the room, David, Rachel and Joe were burned out. And I'd feel better if she were away from all this, so she'll rest."

"Sure. I'll tell her Pam will need help with the kids."

"And," Peggy hesitated, "the Masters, if you have that much room."

"Of course. It does look like the east ridge is pretty much burned over. I'm glad to hear they got out in time."

"They drove down through the fire with nothing but the clothes on their backs, Dave. And there's no question their place is gone. The whole, east-foothills area is black and smoldering."

David nodded sadly. "Bill put so much into that pear orchard, and it was just starting to produce. We'll take them home and do what we can to help."

Jonathan returned as David was loading the wagon. "Did you find out anything about Dad?" he asked.

"No, I didn't, Jon. But I'm sure when we get to the ranch, we'll find he's gotten there ahead of us."

They were more than halfway to the ranch when something in a ravine caught David's eye. He pulled the horses up and handed the reins to Jonathan. "Looks like a car went off the road. Hold the horses while I go look."

As he stumbled down the steep bank, he felt a cold chill. His stomach knotted as he picked out the bright blue shape of the pickup truck. It had rolled several times, bouncing off the granite boulders and snarled manzanita.

He heard Jonathan following behind him. "Go back, Jon," he waved. "Go back and take care of the wagon." But he was too late; the boy had seen the truck too.

"Jon." He hugged his nephew close, then turned him gently back toward the road. "Jonathan, I want you to go back up to the wagon. Please. I need you to do that. I'll go on down and see—"

"But it's Dad! Uncle David, it's Dad! I've got a right to go with you!"

So they struggled on, hand in hand, to the battered truck. David reached out to turn Jonathan's face away, but the boy wrenched free. He stared blankly, for an instant, at the truck.

A rock, no more than six inches wide, rested on the twisted body in the flattened cab. A meteor. It had still been hot enough, after crashing through the truck roof, to melt the polyester jacket and sear the flesh. Jonathan let his uncle hold him, as David, too, turned away.

THE REVELATION

They stood for several moments in silence. Then, realizing that one of the Masters' children had just joined them, David and Jonathan started back up the bank. "We have to go on home now."

"But we can't just leave him here." Jonathan struggled to hold back his tears.

"I'll come back later, Jon, with some help. We'll come back . . . and bring your father home."

8

Pam held little Beth Turner in her lap. Stephanie and Keith Turner sat stiffly between her and David in the church pew, not yet really understanding what had happened. Pam looked past the three caskets and the pulpit to the redwood grove beyond. The treetops were still green, despite the charred underbrush; but the hills were seared, black and bare.

Three days, she thought. *In less than three days my sister has been widowed, and these tiny ones have been orphaned. Our valley has been laid waste. Our valley! Our hemisphere!*

For, as the world rotated on its axis, most of the Northern Hemisphere had been exposed to the relentless comet tail of space dust. It had cut a swath of meteorite craters across the earth. The burning pellets, rocks, and boulders had left behind hundreds, perhaps thousands, of smoldering fires.

THE REVELATION

In many places—the Cascades, the Rockies, New England, Scandinavia—forest fires merged into uncontrollable walls of terror. The fruitful plains of the United States, Canada, Russia, the Ukraine, and China became seas of raging flames, promising an unimaginable winter of famine.

Pam gently stroked Beth's hair as she thought of the survivors. Only a handful of lives had been lost in Little Valley, and these precious ones who had died, she knew, belonged to the Lord. They were with him now, spared the horror that might still be coming.

But the memory of the past days still wrenched sobs from deep within her. She thought of the three Turner children—first fatherless, then told that Mommy, too, had gone to be with Jesus. *Why did that particular meteorite fall in that particular spot on that particular bedroom? How could our merciful God permit these things?* Pam pondered.

And there was no way she could spare Sandy from *her* pain either. No one had to tell Sandy about Bob. She saw the tired horses plod into the yard, dragging the clumsy wagon. Bob was not in it. She saw Jonathan drop slowly from his seat next to David and walk to her, his shoulders sagging, chin low, face streaked with smoke and tears. He looked so small and yet so mature. He walked to her and held out his hands to her. And she knew.

Pam glanced across the aisle to her sister. Sandy sat between her two young sons, shrunken, frail, alone. She had not yet shed a tear, had shown no anger, no fear; she simply had not reacted. *How long,* Pam wondered, *can she sit there, walled off from her*

*family and friends? How long can she survive so
alone? Jesus, don't let her be alone. Be with her, and
help her to let us reach her.*

Frank stepped to the pulpit, and Pam forced her
attention toward him. *He's aged so,* she thought.
Gray had appeared at his temples in the months after
his wife died; but, just since Thanksgiving, he had
become virtually white-haired. Always slender, he was
now gaunt. Events had dug canyons below his deep-
set eyes. His lips were thin, and Pam thought she saw
them tremble.

"Friends," he began with a voice weary and
strained. "Dear friends, we are gathered here today to
praise the Lord." There was a murmur of shock. "You
do not want to praise him today, do you? Neither do I.
We are hurting, and we want to blame him for taking
these three, his children, away from us."

Frank's eyes filled with tears as he looked toward
Sandy and her sons, and then to the Turner children.
"You want to know why he is hurting these little ones
by taking their parents from them. Sandy, you need
your husband, and he is gone."

Art Just grasped Helen's hand, remembering how
they had begged for an answer to that question six
months earlier.

Frank continued his sermon: "I don't know why,
but I do know that Jack and Joan and Bob are with the
Lord today, now! They each expected him to return for
them, and us, before this troubled time—" He stumbled, momentarily. "Before a time like this began.
And the Lord, in a sense, *has* come for them."

"Amen. Praise the Lord," voices responded from the pews.

Frank nodded to those who had interrupted. "Yes, and praise him for this too: Though I don't know how much more we must endure first, He *will* come in all his glory. And when he does, Jack and Joan and Bob will be with him. That certainty is the 'blessed hope of the church.'"

Frank bowed his head and closed the brief service with a prayer—not for those who had died, but for those who still lived.

Half of Little Valley huddled in small, frightened groups in the poppy-studded cemetery. Frank moved from group to group, offering what comfort he could, answering questions when he had the answers, trying to encourage the hopeless to find hope in Christ.

"You really meant that, didn't you, about praising the Lord?" Joe Stenberg asked, puzzled.

"You know that much, Joe, from your own Torah, and from Job and the Psalms."

"I know it is taught, but I don't know anyone who can do it. Though," he wondered out loud, "being with the Cristmans these few hard days, I have seen a peace in them I've never seen before. They do have hope. I'll give them credit for that."

"Not them, Joe. The credit belongs to the Lord. And that hope and that peace is available to anyone."

Joe shrugged and started to turn away. "Not for us, Pastor Thomsen. The God of the Jews is a God of wrath. Our God is the One who is making all this happen."

"He is letting it happen, Joe. That much is true.

But he will show mercy, even now, to those who believe. Why don't you drop by sometime, and we'll talk. I'd like to show you what the prophets said about the time of Jacob's Trouble."

"Maybe, sometime."

Frank moved on. The question he heard most was the one David Cristman broached as Frank lifted a dozing Keith Turner from a front pew.

"Frank, you started to say something a few minutes ago about this 'time.' You covered by saying we were expecting 'a time like this.' But that isn't what you really meant, is it? You think the Tribulation has started, don't you?"

"David, this isn't the time or place to debate interpretations."

"I didn't mean it that way, Frank. Really, I didn't. I've been studying Revelation. Who hasn't? And the first four trumpet judgments—" He shuddered.

"The first four trumpets have often been seen as a comet striking the earth." Frank looked around as if to make sure no one else was listening. "David, all my life I've been taught that he is coming soon, but deep down I can't believe this is the real thing. Still, if that comet does hit, I have to think it will mean the Tribulation has begun."

"Our traditional interpretation puts the Rapture even before the opening of the first seal. Before the war or famine or pestilence. Before any of the trumpets."

"Then our interpretation would appear to be wrong, David."

"There are some who would call that heresy, Frank."

"You?"

"No. My faith doesn't depend on the interpretations of men. I stand on the Word, Frank, even when I don't understand it. And I think that puts us on the same footing."

"It does, David. It does. And thank you for telling me that. I know some of my congregation is questioning my leadership. They think I'm refusing to preach prophecy because I don't believe it anymore. David, I do believe." Frank's hand shook as he grasped David's. "I do believe, but I don't understand. How can I teach them when I don't understand it myself?"

"Pray for wisdom, Frank, and we'll pray with you. And, Frank, if our hope was misplaced, if we are to go through the Tribulation, then Job's affirmation may be the best text you could give us."

Keith stirred in Frank's arms and looked up. As David took the little boy, Frank murmured again the text of last Sunday's sermon. "'Though he slay me, yet will I trust Him.' Thank you, David."

Tom Braden was pressing the same question on Bill Masters as Frank joined them. "So, if this isn't the Great Tribulation, I'd like to know how it could be much worse. And if it is the Tribulation, what happened to the Rapture?"

"Where is the promise of His coming, Tom? Is that what you're asking?" the pastor asked.

"I'm just asking, Pastor, not doubting. I guess I'm a little puzzled."

"It's no sin to doubt, Tom. If we never doubted, we wouldn't need faith."

"Hmmm. Never thought of it that way," Bill muttered

"King David doubted. Job, Peter, even your namesake, Tom, doubted. I've been doing a lot of reading in the Prophets and Revelation the last few months. I don't have many answers. In fact, I have a lot fewer answers than I did before I started studying. I do find, though, that quite a few sound evangelicals over the centuries have expected the church to go through the Tribulation. I'm beginning to think they were right, and we were wrong."

"I never heard of any, Frank. I know our statement of faith includes the pretribulation Rapture, and I never heard of anybody but some fuzzy liberals and modernists who believe otherwise."

"It hasn't been a popular view the past generation or two, Bill. We all want, or wanted, to believe we'd be taken out first. And maybe we will be. Maybe this is only the beginning of the end."

"Christ said the Beast would be revealed first, didn't he?"

"Yes, Bill, he did. And we haven't seen that yet."

"What about Crosetti?" Tom interrupted.

"Maybe, Tom. Maybe he is the Beast, but I don't think we could say he had been 'revealed' as such. No, I think the answer is that we have to wait a little longer. The Word says the prophecies will be clear to those for whom they were meant. I believe he wants us to trust him, to let him work out his will in his time."

"You know, I probably shouldn't admit this. I'm almost ashamed of thinking it, with those three kids all

alone in the world, and Sandy Peters and her boys."
Tom hesitated. "But it is quite a thrill, in a way, to be
seeing so much prophecy fulfilled right before our
eyes. We all talked about the Second Coming. We
accepted it. But, well, we didn't really expect it, did
we, deep down? And here we are, living it."

Bill seemed shocked by Tom's honesty, but Frank
nodded. "It is awesome and terrible, but it is wonderful too, to see such a display of his power and to see, in
the flesh, with our own eyes, the proof of his Word."

"Not for me." Bill shuddered. "I used to pray that
I wouldn't see death, that the Rapture would come in
my lifetime. Now I just hope he lets me die in my
bed."

Bill's wife joined them then and whispered something to her husband. "Will you excuse us, Pastor?"
Bill asked. "We've bought the Peters' motor home to
live in temporarily and are driving up to see what's left
of the homestead. As Wilma suggests, we want a fair
amount of daylight to get settled in."

People were drifting off, now, by twos and threes,
to their homes, or to homes that had been opened to
them. The Masters had offered their car to Sandy in
partial payment for the motor home. David found the
car where it had been parked three days earlier, and
Joe offered to drive Sandy and Pam home in it while
David and the children took the wagon and horses
back up to the ridge.

As Pam prepared supper, with Rachel's help,
David and Joe turned on the television set. This had
already become a ritual. They each had to know what
had happened out there now.

Because the greatest damage from the meteors had been wildfire, the cities had escaped the brunt of the latest disaster. Those towns that had survived the earthquakes and tidal waves of Thanksgiving time were still habitable; so communications, except by satellite, had not been badly disrupted.

There were films from aircraft of the fires that still raged over the northern third of the earth. Most of the planting season was over, but the announcer recited a litany of emergency measures: short season crops that could be planted in the burnt-over land; the use of underdeveloped fertile plains in South Africa and South America; heroic measures already under way in Australia, despite the damage that nation had suffered the past fall.

David listened closely for warning of the disaster he felt was still coming. There was obviously some censorship, though the United Nations denied it strongly. Someone was determined to prevent panic. But the communications blackout was not quite complete.

David heard only a single sentence, but it confirmed his belief that their ordeal was only beginning. "This station continues to receive scattered reports that a few astronomers fear a collision between the earth and the comet itself, but official pronouncements assure us that this will not occur."

Pam had spread sleeping bags and mattresses on the floor in the large back bedroom, turning it into a dormitory for the five children. Joe and Rachel Stenberg obviously could not rebuild their home or relocate until their baby was born, but they had refused the offer of Pam and David's room, insisting on setting up cots in the living room. Sandy had ignored Pam's pleas and shut herself, alone, in the upstairs guest room she had shared with Bob for the past six months.

Most of the occupants of the ranch house were asleep when the impact occurred. It could hardly be called an earthquake; it was unlike any earthquake ever felt by humanity. People would wonder, in the wake of so much destruction, how any structures or any life, for that matter, could possibly have survived.

At the Cristman ranch the old house shook like a rag doll in the mouth of a large, angry dog. David and Pam clung to each other as their bed rocked violently. Joe leaped from his cot to hold Rachel, silently shielding her with his own body as books and bowls flew from the shelves lining the walls.

Mark and Jonathan, thrown from their beds, fell on Stephanie, Keith, and Beth. They all rolled helplessly on the floor among the mattresses, crying. Sandy screamed one agonized word—*Bob*—and began to sob hysterically.

No earthquake shock had ever lasted so long, though it was actually no more than two or three minutes. The redwood framework of the old house stood, but with gaping wounds where there had been windows. The chimney fell, and so did the windmill.

"I do believe God has thrown Satan himself to earth," David breathed, as they surveyed the devastation. "But apparently he means for us to survive, at least for a little while longer."

9

Sandy's sobs subsided within minutes. She sat on the edge of the bed, surveying the damage around her. One of her slippers rested in a shaft of moonlight, skewered to the waxed plank floor by a thin shard of broken glass. She felt for the other and was amazed to find it resting against the leg of the bed. Slipping it on, she hopped across the glass-spattered throw rug to the hall door, just as Jonathan opened it.

"Mom!" Her son rushed into her outstretched arms. "Mom, are you hurt?"

"I'm all right, Jon. I'm all right now. Mark?"

"We're both in one piece," he assured her as they hurried to the children's room. "But I think a couple of the little kids might be hurt."

Pam reached the room just ahead of them with a lantern and was comforting little Beth, who cried as she held her right arm awkwardly at her side. "I'm afraid it's broken, Sandy. What do you think?"

Sandy took the toddler's hand and gently bent it. Beth's scream confirmed the diagnosis. "I need bandages and something solid for a splint." Pam was relieved to realize her sister was her usual competent self again.

"Jonathan," said Pam, "get the first aid kit, please. It's in the bathroom linen closet." She laughed nervously. "David always said a ranch has to have a good first aid kit. As if that could cure everything."

"Aunt Pam." Mark tugged at her nightgown as Sandy concentrated on holding Beth's injured arm still. "Aunt Pam, Keith went to sleep again, and I can't wake him up."

Terror crowded upon terror as Pam knelt by the little boy. He was breathing regularly and didn't appear to be hurt. "Keith, Keith, honey, wake up." But the boy didn't stir. She touched his face, then turned his head away from her and saw the ugly knot just behind his ear. "Concussion, Sandy. Now what?"

Sandy turned Beth over to Mark and knelt beside her sister. She touched the bump gingerly. "I only took a six-week first aid course, Pam. We need a doctor for this."

"Not likely we'll get one. There will be too many injured in town. Can't you do anything?"

"Keep him quiet. Watch him. Pray. Do a lot of praying."

Stephanie had been watching the two women, eyes wide with wonder and fear. "Is Keith going to heaven too, like Mommy and Daddy?"

"No, Stephanie. Keith is just asleep. But his head is hurt, and you must let him sleep for a little while." Pam lifted him tenderly and laid him on the bed that had been Mark's.

Jonathan returned with the first aid kit, and Sandy turned to splint Beth's broken arm. "I think I have things under control here, Pam. Why don't you take Stephanie downstairs and check on the others?"

David had left Pam at their bedroom door and gone to look for damage. He met Joe at the foot of the stairs. "Is Rachel all right?" asked David.

"She seems to be okay. The others? We heard Sandy scream."

"Shock, evidently. Pam listened at her door. She was crying for Bob, but I think that's good. She's been too quiet since—"

"Yes, you're right. I was going up to check on the children," said Joe.

"Pam's with them."

Rachel had wrapped a blanket around herself and joined Joe and David. "I'll go up and—" She gasped suddenly, and put a hand on her back. "I'll go up and help her."

Both men noticed the gesture. "Skip the stairs for now, Rachel," Joe protested. "Pam will call if she needs help."

"He's right, Rachel. You just lie down and take care of yourself." David tried to sound casual as he continued. "We really haven't time to deliver a baby today. Joe, could you prowl around the house and take note of what needs fixing right away? I've got to check outside."

THE REVELATION

Pam stopped in the living room where Rachel was kneeling, stacking some scattered books. "Did Joe go out with David to check for damage?" Pam asked.

"He's checking the house. Are the children all right? I can go up and look after them," Rachel offered.

"Sandy's with them. Beth has a broken arm, but Keith is unconscious." She glanced down at Stephanie, who clung to her hand. "Rachel, Keith may be seriously hurt. If you'd just keep Stephanie occupied here, that would be a big help."

"I'm fine, Pam. Don't feel you have to pamper me."

"Why did you wince when you stood up? Rachel, are you in labor?"

"Of course not. I just had a little cramp in my back. I'm not due for weeks yet."

"Well, maybe. But anyhow, I know where things are and what's most likely to need doing. So, if you'll keep Stephanie down here while Sandy tends to Beth and Keith, I'll take a look at my kitchen."

Jonathan bounded down the stairs then, with the proverbial resilience of youth. "Mom says to get a broom and help you sweep up, Aunt Pam. She's got Beth quieted down, and she says not to fret about Keith. She thinks he'll come around soon; she's going to stay with them. And Mark's cleaning up the mess upstairs."

An hour later they all gathered in the kitchen for cold cereal and fresh milk and to compare notes on the damage. David, at the head of the pine trestle table, bowed his head at Pam's nod. "Father, we thank you that all of our lives have been spared in this, your judgment. We know many have lost their loved ones and many are injured, and we do ask for your mercy. Give us your strength to repair our damages, and your healing for the injured children upstairs. And, Father, glorify your name and the name of Jesus in this time of trouble. Amen."

"You people believe all these disasters are fulfillments of the ancient prophecies, don't you?" Joe asked, as he passed the pitcher of lukewarm milk to Sandy.

"Yes, we think so," David answered hesitantly. "There are so many parallels, especially with the book of Revelation."

"I see similarities with some of the prophets too, of the time before the coming of the Messiah. But since so many thousands of years have passed, I find it hard to believe these things could be happening in our lifetime."

"Even that was predicted, though." David smiled encouragement as he answered. "Men would ask where is the promise of his coming."

"But I thought you believed he had already come."

"Yes, Joe. We believe he came, and was rejected. Isaiah and the Psalms teach that."

"But Isaiah and the others predicted he would reestablish David's kingdom. Your Jesus certainly didn't do that."

"But he will. That is the Second Coming—what we think will happen soon."

"So you believe this judgment is the one we have

been expecting since, I guess, the destruction of Jerusalem in A.D. 70? And you believe that the Messiah is coming to establish our kingdom, just as many of us hope?"

"That's right, Joe."

"Then what is this talk I hear about something called a 'rapture'?" Rachel asked.

David glanced at the long list of needs and repairs he had intended to talk over with his family and guests at breakfast. But he sensed the importance of the Stenbergs' questions. "Many Christians do believe in what we call the Rapture of the church. That is, that Jesus, before the seven years of Tribulation that usher in the Jewish kingdom, will come in the clouds, and the Christians will be taken up to be with him for those seven years in heaven."

"But if this period is part of that seven years— Daniel's seventieth week—then that didn't happen."

"Right, Joe. If this is the Tribulation, and it does look like it, then apparently we were wrong about the Rapture."

"Your Bible was wrong?"

"No. That couldn't be, because it is the Word of God. But our interpretation of some of the prophecies would have to be wrong, if this is the Tribulation."

Rachel was silent, but her busy eyes looked intently at her husband as he spoke his and her thoughts. "Just as—if your Jesus was the Messiah— our Scriptures were right, but our teachers misinterpreted some of the prophecies?"

David nodded as he silently whispered a prayer for guidance. But what Joe needed now was time.

"That's something I'll have to think about, David. But right now we have a lot to do, and you already have a list. Where do we start?"

"Pam's worried about her freezer full of food, and she's right. We can't afford to let that much of our food supply spoil, especially with half of the canned stuff broken. So the wind generator has to be first on the list, Joe, and that will take you, me, and Jonathan the rest of the day, I expect."

"Thank God it's nearly summer," Sandy said. "Things like windows can wait a while."

Pam added, "We'll need the stove, though, for cooking." She glanced at Rachel and noticed a shadow of pain cross her face again, but Rachel insisted she was fine. "And for warmth too, at night, for the children especially."

"Right," David said. "That's next on my list. Maybe we can get the chimney back up after we finish the windmill. We can work on that tonight by lantern light if we have to."

He turned to Sandy. "How was Keith doing when you came down?"

"I wish I knew. He's breathing okay, and his color is good. He just looks like he's sleeping. I told Mark to call me right away if he noticed any change. Do you think we should send Jon to town for a doctor?"

"I'm afraid it might be a waste of time, Sandy. I'm worried about Keith too, but I don't think we should move him. And there are only two doctors left in town. We can't expect one to come all the way out here to look at one child when there must be dozens, maybe hundreds, in town who need him. If there's no change in an hour or two, maybe we can send Jonathan.

"Yes, David. You're probably right."

Sandy looked toward the door as she heard Mark's footsteps on the stairs. "How is Keith, Mark?"

"I can't see any difference, Mom. But Beth is crying because her arm hurts."

"Thanks, Mark. I'll come up and give her another aspirin."

Mark was sent to the spring for water since the pump, too, was electric. David, Joe, and Jonathan gathered their tools and went to rebuild the windmill frame. Rachel started to clear the table. But when a sharp cry escaped her clasped lips, Pam questioned her again. "Are you in labor?"

"Maybe, Pam. I've been having pains every half hour or so, ever since the quake. I'm afraid they're getting closer together."

"How close?"

"I don't know. Maybe fifteen minutes since the last one."

Pam gave her a sharp look.

"Okay, maybe ten. I'm sorry, Pam. This is a terrible time to have a baby. I'm being such a bother to you all."

"Don't be silly, Rachel. Babies are wonderful. They are life, and hope. I envy you." A random thought flashed through her mind: *I do envy her, but perhaps it was a blessing, really, that David and I couldn't have children.*

"Besides," Pam continued, "you didn't *plan* on

having it today. Now I'm taking you upstairs to our room and putting you to bed."

They met a smiling Sandy on the stairs. "Keith just regained consciousness! He's a little confused, but I think he's going to be all right, thank God."

"Thank God," Pam agreed. "And now we have another patient for you, Nurse."

"What do you mean by that?"

Sandy looked at Rachel and then at Pam. "I took a camp counselors' first aid class. It didn't include midwifery. Now we have to send Jon for a doctor, for sure."

David agreed to send Jonathan. "But as long as he's going to town, send some cheese and milk with him. He can try to trade it for flour, salt, sugar, seeds. Money might not be worth much right now."

Jonathan returned about noon with a sack of wholewheat flour and a bagful of vegetable-seed packets. "Mr. Downing said he didn't have any left. He said people were just coming in and taking stuff, and he even had a gun. But when I said I had cheese and milk to trade, he took me into the back room and gave me this stuff."

"Good boy, Jon. Those seeds could keep us alive next year." David regretted immediately that he'd used such strong words. There was no need to terrify the children more than they already were. "When is the doctor coming?" he continued, as Rachel cried out from upstairs.

"I couldn't find a doctor, Uncle David. I went to the office, but it was all messed up from the earthquake. No one had cleaned up anything. Then I went to the hospital, and part of the roof had fallen in, and they had people out on the lawn, like during the fires. I asked everyone for a doctor to come and help. I said Mrs. Stenberg was having her baby, like you said, but they just told me the doctors were all too busy. I tried, Uncle David."

"I know you tried, Jon."

There was a scream from the bedroom. "Go help Mark take care of the little kids," David suggested, to distract the boy from Rachel's agony.

David went upstairs too, and opened the door a crack. "I'm afraid we didn't get a doctor," he said softly.

"I don't think we need one now," Pam answered, turning from the bed. She placed a blanket-wrapped bundle in Joe's arms as she went to the door to speak to David. "It's a boy—a beautiful, healthy boy."

Rachel's face was white within the halo of her damp, black curls, but she smiled. "David, I'd like to introduce our son, Daniel."

10

"**D**o you have any idea what time it is, David?" Pam rolled over on the cot in the living room and picked up her watch from the floor. "This thing says it's two o'clock."

"A.M. or P.M.?" David got up and opened the makeshift shutters on the window. It's gray out there, but it's been gray ever since the meteorites. I guess that's to be expected, with fires all over the hemisphere."

"But what I don't understand is why it gets dark, really dark, so soon, and then light again, more or less. I know I haven't slept eight hours. I didn't last night. The days are shorter. I know they are. Days *and* nights."

"It sure seems like it. The clocks are haywire anyhow, but all our watches seem to agree pretty well, and yet—" David shook his head, puzzled. "You know, if that comet did hit the earth, it could have speeded up the rotation or something like that."

"I was wondering about that too," Joe interjected, as he came down the stairs. "Does your Bible mention that?"

"As a matter of fact, it does." David turned on a light and opened his Bible. "It says that after the rain of hail and fire, and the burning up of all the grasses, there will be a massive rock thrown into the ocean, and the sun and moon will each be darkened by one-third. We always thought this referred to darkness from the smoke, just like the moon turning to blood seems to refer to the red color it picks up. But maybe it means more."

"Rachel and I have been talking, Dave. If a prophet prophesies things that actually happen, it is a sign that he is a prophet of God. We think, perhaps, this John was a true prophet after all."

Pam smiled up at him. "You see, all things work for good. This has been such a week of terror, and yet now you have a fine baby boy, and you are learning more about the Lord."

He answered gently, "We want to know more, but maybe you Christians are right. If this is Sunday, and who knows with the time all messed up, I'd like to go to church with you. Your pastor told me to feel free to ask more questions."

"Ask away. We'll help all we can, and so will Frank." Pam turned to her husband. "Shall we try to get ourselves together and take the wagon into town, David? No one knows what time it is, and I doubt there'll be any formal service, but we should find out how our friends are doing."

"I'd been thinking the same thing," Sandy said, as she and the boys joined them. "From what Jon said Wednesday, there is a lot of damage in town. People will need help. And if ever we all needed Christian fellowship, this is the time."

"How are our invalids?"

"What invalids!" Sandy smiled as she continued. "Rachel's nursing Daniel. He's a little guy, but he sure has a good appetite. I can hardly keep Keith or Beth in bed. I can stay home, just in case, but there's no reason the rest of you shouldn't go visiting."

"Me too, Mom? I want to see what happened in town."

"Of course, Mark. You, and Jonathan too, if he wants to go."

Pam cried when she saw what was left of the little church. When it escaped the fires she'd felt it was a protected shelter, but now it was shattered. The lofty A-frame had toppled intact to one side and then collapsed.

The pews still stood inside the cement block foundation. The pulpit still stood at the front of the choir platform. And Frank Thomsen stood behind the pulpit, head bowed, as David drew the horses to a halt.

Frank heard them as they climbed down from the hay wagon, and he lifted his head. His tear-stained face cracked into a smile as he walked toward Pam and David, arms outstretched. "I haven't the foggiest idea what time it is, but I gather you folks think it's time for church."

"Then it isn't just our clocks and watches."

"Whole world's gone crazy, Pam. Whole town and whole world." He glanced to the wagon where Joe and the boys were tending the horses. "How badly were you people hit?"

"Not badly, actually." As David's eyes took in the town's extensive damage, he realized just how much God had protected his own household. "Sandy is home nursing Keith and Beth, who were slightly injured in the quake. And Rachel had a baby boy night before last."

"A boy." Frank turned to Joe. "Congratulations, then. So life still goes on, amid all the death."

The Cristmans' arrival had not gone unnoticed by the town. People moved, cautiously and wearily, out of the buildings that still stood and gathered in the grove behind the ruined church. Pained smiles greeted the good news from the ranch.

"Jon came to me at the hospital for help, Pam," Peggy Braden tried to apologize. "We were just so overwhelmed. There were so many hurt, so many screaming for help. And only two doctors left."

"We understood, Peggy."

"I couldn't leave, Pam, and there was no one else to send. I hated turning him away."

"You don't have to justify yourself to me, Peggy. I know you did all you could. And we made out fine."

"But how? Jonathan said Keith was unconscious . . . and Rachel, with the baby?"

"Sandy's had some first aid training; but mostly,

the Lord was with us. Funny how often we say that, but it's really true. Keith just woke up, on his own, and Rachel had a perfectly normal delivery."

"Wasn't the baby early?"

"Only two or three weeks. He's not real big, but he seems perfect, and she's got lots of milk too."

"Praise the Lord!"

"For what?" Tom spoke bitterly to his wife. "Praise God for what? The town levelled. Half the people hurt. Dozens dead. He promised he would come for us. He promised the church would be saved from all this."

"All what, Tom?"

"Don't try to *comfort* me, Frank. If this isn't the Tribulation, how do you explain it? Revelation 8. The first four trumpets. Well, I believed. That was supposed to mean I was saved. And the saved were supposed to be raptured out of the Tribulation."

"Tom, Tom, don't take out your fears on the pastor or our friends."

"Shut up, Peg. You know it's all been a lie. They're all liars. God is a liar."

Pam and David drew away, grateful that Joe and the boys had drifted off to talk to other friends, missing Tom's harsh words. "I don't see Art or Helen, Pam. Let's head up toward their place."

They picked their way across the burned-over lots and past sagging buildings. One wall of the Justs' modern redwood-and-glass house had crumpled, and the roof drooped forlornly. Windows gaped, not yet boarded over. But Tammy sat on the warped deck, grubby hands grasping a peanut-butter-covered soda cracker.

Pam stooped. "Where are your grandma and grandpa, Tammy?"

"There." She pointed to a shattered sliding door.

"Anybody home?" David called, as he pulled out the remaining fragments of glass and stepped inside. The once gracious, always immaculate living room was littered, not just with broken glass and plaster, but with dirty plates and empty food cans. The cracker box sat on Helen's glass-topped coffee table. A knife smeared with peanut butter lay beside it. "Art? Helen? Jimmy?"

"What do you want? Oh, David, it's you." Art groped his way from the next room. "Glasses got broken, and I can't see much without them."

"It looks like the quake hit you pretty hard. We saw Tammy outside. Are Helen and Jimmy all right?"

Art Just had become an old man in the past six months. He had to think a few minutes before answering. "Jimmy? Yes, Jimmy. He was in there." Art's voice shook as he pointed to the collapsed roof. "They came and dug him out. They took him. Helen went to find him."

David tried to grasp what Art was trying to say. "Helen was hurt, Art?"

"No. She wasn't hurt. She was in our room, with me. But she went to find Jimmy," Art replied slowly.

"Tammy just told me her grandmother is at the cemetery, David." Pam had just walked in, and looked from Art to the filthy room. "Art," she insisted quietly. "Art, where is Helen?"

"I told you. Jimmy was under the roof," he mumbled. "They dug out his body and buried it with the others. Our little Jimmy, in a mass grave. Our little Jimmy." His eyes wandered to the broken window, and he stared emptily past the shattered glass.

"Jimmy went to heaven, like Mommy and Daddy." Tammy reached for another cracker, and Pam spread it for her.

"Did your grandma go to heaven too, Tammy?" David prodded.

"No," the little girl insisted. "Grandma went to the cemetery."

"David, I'm going to clean up some of this mess and get Tammy a decent meal. Why don't you try to find someone who knows what really happened."

"I was just going to suggest that. We can't leave Art here alone like this, with Tammy."

David did find Helen at the cemetery; Tammy had been right. Helen sat alone, slumped upon the packed earth that marked Little Valley's first mass grave. She had been robbed of the chance to properly mourn her children. Now all her sorrow focused on this one grave. Like her husband, she was in shock.

She didn't protest when David took her hands and lifted her to her feet. She put one foot in front of the other, mechanically, as he led her back to what was left of her house.

Pam had worked a minor miracle. Tammy and Art sat on the couch eating corned beef sandwiches and drinking canned grapefruit juice. Art looked up as David led Helen into the room. "Did you find him?"

She shook her head. "I found the place. They said they put him with the others. All of my children gone, and no markers. No place to put flowers."

"We can't leave the Justs here like this, David. They're helpless children, all three of them."

David nodded. "Art, we're going to take you out to the ranch for dinner—you, Helen, and Tammy. Is that all right? Pam's going to pack some clothes for you, and we'll take you home with us."

They had just started packing the Justs' clothing when Frank called through a broken bedroom window. "Dave? Pam? Joe said you had come up here."

David stepped outside. "Frank, Art and Helen are both in shock. There is no way they can look after themselves, let alone Tammy. We thought we'd take them back to the ranch for a while."

"You can't carry the weight of the world, David. I've been looking in on them every few hours. You're stunned by the mess and the lack of food and sanitation. But we're all in the same condition, really, here in town. I have no running water, and no means of cooking either. We can't all move to your ranch. We're surviving, and we will survive as long as the Lord lets us."

"Well, what do you think now, Frank?" Dave asked. "Is this the Tribulation? Were we wrong about the Rapture? Or did we just miss it? Or—?"

"Or is Tom Braden right? Did we believe a lie?"

"No, Frank," Dave protested. "I know Tom is wrong. God is God, and he can't lie. As you said the day of the funerals, there always were some who believed the church would go through the Tribulation. They must have been right."

Frank sighed and looked toward the Justs. "Maybe we were wrong about the pretribulation Rapture, but I don't know if the others were right either. I don't know anything right now. I'm the pastor. I'm the one they come to for answers, and I don't have any."

"Joe and Rachel are being drawn to Jesus by this."

"Yes." Frank stood a bit taller and lifted his bowed head in hope. "I just had a long talk with Joe."

"Has he trusted the Lord yet? Does he believe, now, that Jesus is the Messiah?"

"Not quite. But he said John filled the criteria for a true prophet, and he's going to read what else he had to say. You and your family have been a tremendous witness to him, David."

"Are we ready to go?" Pam came out on the deck, two small suitcases in her hands.

"I'll take on this case, Pam. At least I can do that much." Frank took the suitcases from her. "Helen and Art will be all right once they get over the shock. I'll take them over to my place for a few days. It's in a little better shape than this."

Unbelievably, the sun was already well down toward the horizon when they got the Justs settled into Frank's study. Hurrying back to the church, Pam and David were surprised to find Joe reading what looked like a newspaper.

"Where did that come from? What does it say?"

Joe held the tattered tabloid-sized sheet out to David. "Somebody with an old hand press up in Sonora managed to team up with a ham operator who has a generator. A fellow trying to get back to his family in Eureka traded this copy for a few gallons of gas."

The little paper contained nothing that could be called solid news. It reported rumors, gathered from a network of ham operators and frightened travelers. The earthquake, it said, had decreased in intensity as one moved eastward. More tidal waves had drenched the West Coast, moving up to twenty miles inland, where the coast ranges didn't block them.

Reports were coming in of millions of dead fish left behind, rotting on the beaches. Wildfires still burned in parts of the Midwest. And frightening stories of diseases, spread by contaminated water, were beginning to appear already.

"And did you notice the little story down in the corner?" Joe asked David. "The one about the secretary general?"

"Yes." David turned to include Pam in the discussion. "Crosetti was surveying fire damage in central Germany and his plane crashed. He's in a hospital on life support. The report is that he is brain dead, but his doctors haven't turned off the machines."

Pam gasped. "The death stroke, David? The death stroke of the Beast?"

11

Jonathan mopped his sweaty forehead with his sleeve and cupped his hand over his eyes as he looked up toward the sun. No one ever knew what time it was anymore. David had been right about the collision with the comet speeding the earth's rotation, but now the days were gradually lengthening as the rotation slowed again.

At the ranch, lunch was served whenever the sun reached its zenith. Jonathan was tired and hungry. He'd spent several hours hoeing the oversized garden where the seeds he'd gotten a few weeks earlier had already begun to sprout.

He decided it must be nearly lunch time. He pulled his work gloves off, picked up the hoe, and was heading back toward the house when he heard a distant buzzing. Turning, he saw what looked like a large swarm of bees whirling across the pasture. *Good*, he thought. *Uncle David has been worrying about enough bees to pollinate the corn.*

As Jonathan skirted the edge of the pasture, he whistled, and Patsy sauntered over to have her head scratched. Even the collie was working overtime now, guarding the precious milk cows, while the men finished rebuilding the barn the earthquake had destroyed. As Jonathan pulled a few cockleburs from her dense coat, Patsy lifted her ears and eyed the approaching swarm.

The buzzing insects almost seemed to be following him, Jon noticed apprehensively. He hurried toward the ranch house. When he leaned his hoe against the porch rail, the first few "bees" reached him. But he quickly realized they were not bees at all.

Like most boys, he was more fascinated than frightened by creeping or flying things. He reached out to catch one for a closer look. It was about the size of a grasshopper, but its hard shell had a golden glitter. Its head had two tiny beads for eyes and was covered with fine, hairy feelers. Jonathan had very little time to admire its striking appearance, though, before it stung him viciously on the palm of his outstretched hand.

Sandy heard his scream and rushed to the kitchen door. "Jon, what's wrong?" She could see the insects swarming around the boy on the porch.

"Don't open the screen, Mom," he sobbed. "They sting bad."

Sandy quickly grabbed the milk can she had been washing. She filled it with water and splashed the cold liquid through the screen toward Jonathan, causing most of the insects to retreat in all directions. He picked off the few that remained on his body, then edged in past the partly open screen door.

Tears streamed down his face, though he struggled to hold them back. As his mother reached out to touch him, he pulled away in pain. Sandy gasped at the sight of his swollen face and arms.

David and Joe had heard Jonathan's cries from the barn and, as they ran toward the house, saw the scattering insects. "Rachel took the kids on a hike in the woods, didn't she, Joe? Better go warn her to bring them in the other door. Looks like we've got a swarm of bees."

Joe detoured widely toward the woods at the front of the house. David buttoned his shirt collar high and stepped cautiously across the graveled parking area between the barn and house. He felt something hard pelt against the back of his neck, and he slapped at it.

"Ouch!" The sharp pain seemed to travel instantly from his neck all the way to his toes; his eyes filled suddenly with tears. "Oooh, that smarts," he shuddered. "Careful not to let any inside," he warned Pam, who held the screen part way open for him.

The luxury of using energy to make ice had been given up at the ranch house, so Sandy was bathing Jonathan's face and hands with cool, spring water. He'd stopped trying not to cry. "Uncle David, what are they?" he asked through his tears. "I thought it was a swarm of bees, but it wasn't. I never saw anything like them."

"Neither have I, Jon."

"Is this the plague of locusts we've been expecting, do you think?" Pam asked. The dead creature from David's neck lay in the sink, and she turned it over carefully with a long meat fork.

"Another symbol that wasn't meant to be a symbol?" David, too, leaned over to study the insect corpse. "You know, it's really beautiful in a strange sort of way. Shiny gold, hard. I'm surprised I managed to kill it with my hand. Look at the feelers around its head, like long hair. Two eyes, a mouth, and the stinger in the tail."

"Don't be silly." Sandy turned and reached for the first aid kit. "Even if this is the Tribulation, the locusts aren't supposed to bother the sealed. Jonathan has accepted the Lord. And . . . if you aren't a Christian, David, who is?"

"But who were the sealed ones, Sandy? Revelation says they were Jews. If these are literal locusts, could be the sealed are literal Jews, maybe."

The conversation was punctuated by the chatter of the children whom Rachel now herded upstairs to wash for lunch. As Joe came into the kitchen, he, too, gasped at the sight of Jonathan, whose sobs had finally subsided from utter exhaustion. "Oh, Jon, you poor kid. Those bees really got to you, didn't they?"

"Except they aren't bees, Joe. Come look at this thing."

Joe whistled as he looked down into the sink, then stopped short. "Strangest looking bug I've ever seen, Dave. Do you suppose it's some kind of mutation from the comet's radiation? There was something on the news a couple of days ago."

"I thought I heard them say something about some plague of insects," Pam said. "But you know the news is so sketchy these days, all coming from the UN like it does."

"Somebody doesn't want to start a panic." Sandy laughed hoarsely. "Someone thinks what is really happening is actually worse than imagination or rumor."

"Maybe he, or they, are right about that." David took a damp cloth from Pam's hand and daubed at his neck again. "Maybe they're right."

The following Sunday, Jonathan's eyes were still swollen shut. His lips were so tender he couldn't eat solid food, though he didn't seem actually ill. Sandy insisted on staying home with him, but Pam dressed the younger children for church.

As David hitched the horses to the trusty hay wagon, he reached up every few minutes to rub the festering bite on his neck.

"Have you any idea how lucky you are to have that wagon and the horses, Dave?" Joe asked, hanging up the last of the shiny milk pails he'd been washing.

"Sure do, Joe. The Lord has been very good to us."

"And to Rachel and me for sending you to us. What would we have done without your help? You took us in, fed us, delivered our baby. How could I ever repay you?"

"By doing what you're doing, helping with the work. With Bob gone, this place would have been unmanageable without you." David smiled, realizing how true his own statement had been. "So the Lord provided us for each other. Anyhow, we did it because it was necessary, not to be repaid."

Joe seemed to be searching for words. "It was necessary for you, because you have a loving nature, just as it was necessary to God's loving nature that the Christ die for our sins."

David turned, then, to look at his friend. "You believe that now, don't you?"

"Yes, David. It was hard to accept, hard to understand. But living here with you and Pam and Sandy has shown us a very different Christianity than we'd ever seen before. And of course, there are these prophecies being fulfilled so quickly, right before our eyes. Rachel and I intend to confess our faith publicly today, but we wanted you to know first."

David grasped Joe's hands firmly. "That's wonderful! That's the most wonderful thing I've heard in, well, years I think. Pam and Sandy will be delighted too."

That morning the entire congregation burst into a chorus of Hallelujahs as Joe and Rachel stepped forward in response to Pastor Frank's altar call. After the service these two new Christians found themselves surrounded by old friends who were now "family."

But the joy was dampened by news of the latest troubles. Pam had noticed Tammy's puffy red arm, as the little girl sat next to her grandfather. "We had a little cortisone ointment on hand, and that seemed to help, but we couldn't get any more," Art explained.

"Art, we used cold water first, but then Sandy thought about trying a mint tea; it's really given

Jonathan a lot of relief. He was covered with stings. He's still rather uncomfortable, but at least he's gotten some sleep and the swelling is starting to go down."

"I don't know of anyone in town who's tried that. We haven't seen swarms of them, like you were talking about, but most every family's got someone with one or two stings. Helen has a couple on her face."

"Is that why she's not here today?" Frank asked, joining the group.

"Ah, yes, that's why." Art hesitated. "She has a bite on her lip, and it's pretty painful."

"Tell her I'll drop by later, then."

"Well, maybe that's not too good an idea, Pastor." Art shrugged, and then continued. "To be honest, she's not very good company lately. She's so angry. She can't understand why God is letting these things happen to people who trusted him. She's been saying terrible things."

"I've heard a good many terrible things in my day, Art. Maybe I could say something to help."

"I don't think she'd listen to you. She says these things, these locusts, are satanic."

"So do a great many other people, Art. I think so myself, in fact."

"But Helen seems to think that they have won." Art glanced around to see who else might hear as he confessed, reluctantly, "Helen is convinced Satan has defeated God."

Pam gasped in horror, and Frank shuddered as he tried to reassure Art. "I'm sure she doesn't really believe that. Helen has had a real testimony. She knows the Lord. She's just discouraged. She was terribly hurt by Jimmy's loss. I'll come over and talk to her."

"Come if you like," Art sighed. "But Helen is sure the God she believed in would never permit his children to suffer like this. I'm so afraid for her, Pastor. I'm so afraid for all of us."

"These are frightening times, certainly," Rachel said, gently patting the old man's arm with one hand while cradling Daniel in the other. "But the Lord has given us such peace since Joe and I have come to trust him. We do not understand what is happening, but we do trust that everything is coming about just as he planned. We marvel at the fulfillment of the prophecies."

"As you see them, Rachel," Art said. "But you haven't been taught all the things we have. You weren't expecting the Rapture, so you aren't disappointed that it hasn't happened before all this. And now the locusts, and no sealing. The Christians were supposed to be sealed!"

"I never realized it before, but that's basically inconsistent."

"What's inconsistent, Pam?"

"The idea that the Christians wouldn't be tortured by the locusts, considering the Christians were supposed to have been raptured already, anyhow, Art."

"Oh, you know about that. The ones who are sealed are the saved of the Tribulation."

"Now I'm really confused," Rachel interrupted. "You thought everyone who was already a believer would suddenly be taken away, but then more would believe, without witnesses, and those new believers wouldn't be stung by the locusts?"

Rachel's questions suddenly sounded obvious, and Frank was grateful for her innocence. "You see, Art, Rachel has peace. She is being delivered from the Tribulation, spiritually, because as a new Christian she has no preconceived ideas of what God ought to be doing or how."

"She's just taking the Word at face value." Pam hugged Rachel affectionately as she concluded. "Rachel and Joe can teach us all what real faith, child-like faith, is all about."

12

Pam closed the Bible and laid it on the table. "Don't stop now, Aunt Pam," Keith protested. "We want to hear how Joseph gets out of the dungeon."

Pam smiled down at his and Stephanie's upturned faces, and at Beth, curled into a ball on the rug in front of the stove. "Not now, Keith. Beth's already asleep, and you and Stephanie have to have your baths and be tucked in before Pastor Frank gets here for Bible study."

Beth stirred and rubbed a chubby arm across the welt on her cheek. "Hurt," the little girl moaned. Pam stooped and lifted Beth, who winced again as she woke. "Mommy, my face hurts."

Mommy. The word sang in Pam's ears. "I'll get some medicine for it, darling. Now let's all go upstairs to bed." She cradled Beth, though the three year old was getting too heavy to carry far.

Stephanie ran ahead, but Keith clung to Pam's free hand. "Please, can I have some medicine too? I got bit on my leg this afternoon."

"Oh, God," Pam whispered. "Oh, God, why are you letting this happen to these babies? They're so innocent. You say you love them. But you've taken their parents away from them. You've put them into this crowded house where they all have to sleep in one bed in a room with two other children. Won't you at least protect them from the stings?"

She rubbed, absently, at the lump on her own hand. "At least spare the children if you won't spare us all."

The extract of wild mint that Sandy had concocted did seem to help. Pam bathed Beth's cheek, Keith's leg, and her own hand. Then she gave each child a hug and tucked the patchwork quilt around them. Bending, she planted a kiss on each forehead.

The children had already fallen asleep. Stephanie, almost six, slept with her curly head pillowed in one hand; Keith, just four, sprawled on his stomach, nose barely sticking out for air; and Beth had her thumb in her mouth again.

Oh, Lord, I love them so. Pam recalled the sadness of the day she and David had learned they could not have children of their own. *I would thank you for them, if only . . . no, I do thank you, Lord, that we were here to take them in when they needed us.*

As she went downstairs she heard a knock at the door and realized Frank had arrived for their regular Tuesday Bible study.

Sandy opened the door, smiling. "Come in out of

that rain, Frank, and let me hang your coat by the kitchen stove to dry. Rachel and Joe are upstairs getting Daniel settled for the night, and here's Pam, now." Sandy hurried to the kitchen with the wet raincoat and gave a quick tap to the Chinese gong that hung just outside the back door.

David, in the barn, heard the gong and tossed a last forkful of hay into the manger. "You boys about done straining that milk?" he called to his nephews. "Pastor's here for Bible study."

Frank was even more quiet than usual as the household gathered around the blazing stove. He looked up at each member of the extended family as they entered, but said nothing until all were settled. Then he turned to Sandy's boys. "Jon, I left some papers in my car, and I seem to have dropped my glasses too. Would you and Mark please go get them for me?"

"I'll go, Pastor Frank," Mark offered quickly. "Jon doesn't need to get wet too."

"Better both go, Mark, so one can hold the lantern."

As the boys slipped into their sweaters, Sandy studied Frank's strange insistence that both boys go outside. The door closed behind them, and she asked quickly, "What's wrong, Frank?"

He sighed and looked around the warm circle. "I'm afraid I have some bad news. Tom Braden tried to kill himself yesterday morning." Frank saw his friends' disbelief. "He slashed his throat but missed his jugular."

"He has been terribly depressed ever since the

earthquake," Pam recalled. "He was so sure the Rapture would happen any minute."

"Yes. And working outside like he does, he's been terribly bothered by the locusts." David shook his head sadly. "I know there have been people driven literally crazy by the bites. Was that it, Frank?"

"I'm sure that was part of it, Dave. The pain—" He wriggled, pressing his own shoulder against the back of the Boston rocker. "The pain is so constant. It wears people down. But it was more than that. Peggy said he just gave up."

"Gave up, Frank?" Sandy asked. "What do you mean, if not the locusts?"

"Well, there were the locusts. He'd had to quit work because of the stings. All this rebuilding going on, and a carpenter not working because of insect bites! It's got to be hard to take."

"But we're farming, Frank," David protested. "Sure, the stings are painful, but Joe and I have found if we bundle up good we can avoid them most of the time. And they don't really cause permanent damage."

Frank nodded. "I shouldn't talk, I guess. I can stay inside most of the time. I've only had a few bites. Some people are more sensitive than others too, and Tom is evidently one of those. But there's an element of will too."

"If a person really wants to keep going," Joe offered, "he can go on in spite of the pain. As David says, they don't cause anything but pain."

"As if that weren't enough." Pam thought again of the children.

"Yes, *if* he wants to go on, Joe, and *if* he sees a reason. Tom has lost his hope."

"But Tom has always been so sure the Lord was coming soon." Sandy thought of Bob, who had shared Tom's certainty. "Remember how he pressured you to preach more to the lost because the time was so short?"

"Maybe he was too sure, Sandy. I talked to him a few days ago—that's how much good I seem to be able to do these days. He showed me his Bible. He'd done a very strange thing. He'd cut out all the passages he felt promised the church would not go through the Tribulation. 'There,' he told me. 'Those were all lies. Tell me why I should believe the rest.' "

Though no one actually moved, the little circle seemed to draw tighter. After several moments Pam spoke softly. "You said he tried to kill himself, Frank. How is he?"

"He's in the hospital. He'll recover, physically anyhow. Peggy found him in the bathroom just in time."

"How terrible for Peggy. I'll ride in to see her tomorrow," said Sandy.

"Sandy, I don't think you should."

"But, Frank, she needs her friends now."

"Yes, but I don't think you should go to town alone. There are so many things going on."

"The locusts are no worse there than here."

"The locusts are the least of my worries, Sandy. In fact, they're beginning to disappear."

"That's right. Their five months' reign is almost up, isn't it? So why shouldn't I go to town, Frank?"

"Sandy, it's the people. There are thugs on the streets all the time."

"He's right, Sandy," David agreed. "I don't think any of you women, or any of us for that matter, should go to town alone. There are a lot of hungry people out there."

"Not just hungry ones, either. Mean ones," Joe added. "Several women have been attacked. People have been beaten up for no apparent reason. A few have just disappeared. No one is enforcing any laws anymore. I thank the Lord every day that Rachel and the baby are safe out here."

"And pray they, and all of you, are *kept* safe out here," Frank added. "Tom, and many like him, may have given up, but I'm reminded every day of just how the Lord is protecting his people."

"Amen," David said, the others echoing their amens too. "Just look around us at his providential preparations. We certainly never planned this ranch as a refuge from the Tribulation. We didn't expect to live through it any more than Tom did. But here we are with a good spring, a wind generator, wood for heat and cooking. We have good soil and seeds to plant in it. We have cows for milk for the kids and to trade for things we can't grow."

"And each of us have been led directly here by him," said Sandy. "We left San Jose a day before we'd planned and would have all drowned in the tsunami if Bob—" Sandy noticed Frank's tender smile as her gaze dropped.

"God brought us here to find Christ," said

Rachel. She thought of Daniel, upstairs in his crib. "And to bring Danny safe into this unsafe world."

"Even *our* being here is a miracle," Pam echoed. "David was as surprised as the rest of his family when his grandfather willed this ranch to him. So we all have a lot to thank God for, don't we?" Pam looked around the room at her loved ones and thought, again, of the children upstairs who, every now and then, forgot, and called her Mommy.

"Say, I did bring some good news too," Frank said. "There's a regular TV news broadcast started up from Sacramento. It's on every night at nine o'clock."

"Every night?" Jonathan questioned. "Every night, like it used to be?"

"That's what they tell me. No more trying to catch something accidentally from a satellite that happens to pass our dish when we happen to have the set on."

"Did you say nine o'clock, Frank? It's five minutes to, now." David snapped on the set and fiddled with the dial. Soon he was rewarded with a snowy picture and a voice breaking through loud and clear.

There were reports of good harvests in the southern United States and much of Europe, despite the spring fires. A scientist speculated in an interview that the shortened nights had actually speeded growth of the crops that had been replanted. The United Nations planned distribution as equitably as possible; or so their acting secretary general assured his listeners. They hoped that he was right.

The Cristman household exchanged startled looks as the announcer prepared to sign off the all-too-brief hour. "The Security Council urges each of you, now, to intercede with the deity, by whatever name and in whatever means your culture uses, for the preservation of our world." So, each night after that, they gathered around the box that renewed their contact with what passed for civilization. If they had thought before the time of trouble began that all the news was bad, now they wondered how the reporters seemed always to minimize the suffering in the world.

There was hunger, but the Security Council was preventing starvation. There was crime, but the Security Council was reorganizing police forces. There were scattered wars among small nations in the Orient and Africa, but the Security Council was acting as intermediary.

And nearly every night there was the announcement that the secretary general remained in critical but stable condition in a hospital in Vienna.

"I thought he'd been killed in a plane crash just before the comet collision," Pam had wondered the first time they heard this report.

"So did I," said David.

"Yes, but I heard they were keeping him alive on life-support systems."

"All this time, Frank? Doesn't that seem strange?"

"Not especially. He was a much respected, powerful man. If there were any hope he might recover, I suppose they'd try."

"The Beast will die and return to life."

"Yes, Pam," David agreed. "If Crosetti should suddenly wake up, that would pretty much settle the issue for me."

"Yes, I guess." Frank shook his head slowly in contradiction of his own words. "But no matter how often I read about the Beast, or how the facts line up, I can't quite believe what I'm seeing."

"He's been brain dead for five months. If he should come back to life—" Sandy shuddered. "Frank, could even Satan have that much power?"

"If God permitted it, Sandy. If Crosetti is God's instrument for judgment . . . no, not God's instrument, the devil's. Maybe Satan himself will simply possess the body that was Crosetti's."

"Our Lord took on human flesh," Pam puzzled. "But he was God."

"The more reason Satan would try to do the same." David nodded to his wife. "And God could let him try."

There was no idle speculation the night the announcement came. When they heard it, each one knew, instantly, what it meant. The secretary general, who had lain in a Vienna hospital for five months on life-support equipment with no evidence of brain activity, had suddenly regained consciousness.

His longtime friend, the Reverend Stanley Singer, Chairman of the International Interfaith Council, credited the collective prayers of all mankind—Christian and Jew, Muslim and Buddhist, "all who have called upon their gods on his behalf"—for the trusted leader's miraculous recovery.

Crosetti's recovery was startlingly rapid. Within days, his kindly face appeared on the nightly news report. He grieved for the hardships the world had suffered while he was ill. He assured them that soon dramatic improvements would be at hand, now that he was back in control.

As if to affirm his promise, the vicious locusts disappeared. "Of course, I cannot take the credit for this relief," he told a Thanksgiving Day audience. "Our scientists have been working twenty-four hours a day for the past five months to defeat this enemy, but I am pleased to announce that one of my first acts upon resuming office was to approve the successful mass-spraying effort."

Joe laughed. "He sprayed the whole world in a day, I suppose!"

"I hate to think what really happened."

"What do you mean, David?" Joe asked.

"The king of the locusts is the demon out of the pit. And Crosetti is the prince of demons himself."

Frank, who was sharing the holiday dinner with his friends, shook his head. "Don't you think you might be jumping to conclusions, David?"

"But his healing fits perfectly," Sandy interrupted.

"I know, but Crosetti is known as a devout man, an evangelical. Before his accident he had the support of practically every Christian leader in the world."

"That was before his accident. Frank, the man was dead—brain dead—for five months! Suddenly he wakes up, comes back to life. Surely you understand what that means."

"I know what it might mean, sure. But let me play devil's advocate for a few minutes." He chuckled softly. "Literally, perhaps. I remind you we all *knew* the church was to be raptured before the Tribulation. We *knew* the Lord's servants were to be protected from the locust stings. Dave, when you asked a year ago, right after the Thanksgiving earthquake, if that was the beginning of the Tribulation, I said the more I studied the fewer answers I had. Well, I still feel the same way."

"Okay. I don't know all the answers either, Frank. So I don't know, for sure, but I don't trust Crosetti. And I certainly don't trust Brother Stan, his so-called spiritual advisor."

"We'll all go along with you on that, Dave," Frank agreed. "Stanley Singer's message is the same old half-truth: the love of God without his holiness; his mercy without his justice; his power without his sovereignty. It sounds harmless. It sounds good, as far as it goes. That's what makes Singer's blasphemy so dangerous."

Pam nodded as she turned to the children, who listened in bewilderment to the adult debates that surrounded them. "Come on, Sandy. Help me get these little ones ready for their naps."

Even those who believed Crosetti was actually the Beast of Revelation had to admit conditions were improving rapidly now that he was directing the United Nations again. Rebuilding the Western world's industrial and communications systems sprinted forward. Gasoline became available again. Television expanded from a one-hour newscast each day to full-evening broadcasting, even including substantial religious programming. It was ecumenical programming, to be sure, directed by Singer and his International Interfaith Council. But the gospel had never had such exposure on prime time as it did now.

"Yeah, prime time, right between the Ayatollah from Syria and the daily horoscope," David reminded them.

"The two witnesses at the ruins of Jerusalem are getting plenty of coverage, you must admit, Frank," Sandy insisted one Tuesday evening when the pastor had joined them for Bible study. "And they are winning souls too."

"Yes, Sandy. Praise the Lord they are being effective. And—" Frank grinned at her not-so-subtle reference, "if they are not the two witnesses of Revelation, chapter 11, they're fantastic counterfeits."

"I've certainly been blessed listening to them," Rachel mused quietly. "Especially Brother Jonah. He has made so many things clear to me from the Bible."

"Yes, he's quite a preacher all right. But I'm afraid most people are more interested in Brother Elias's miracles."

"It's not the first time the Lord has used miracles such as fire from heaven and healing to bring people to his Word, Joe. Yes—" David paused. "Yes, the two witnesses, two men preaching at the ancient Wailing Wall. Does this convince you at last, Frank?"

"Two witnesses, representing the Holy Spirit and the Word of God. Perhaps," Frank almost conceded.

"I just wish I knew exactly when they began to preach," David mused. "That's one date I'd like to mark on my calendar."

"You too?" Sandy queried. "I thought I was the only one still trying to set dates."

"There seems to be something in us, most of us anyhow, Sandy, that demands foreknowledge." Frank frowned as he looked at his friends. "I think, myself, that that was the sin of Eve. Satan promised her knowledge, you may recall. But what we all need is much more faith, faith to just live one day at a time, trusting God and only him for the future."

"Have we any choice?" David concluded. "Shall we get back to our study?"

Christmas morning the children got up early to find warm, new, hand-knit sweaters and caps under a freshly cut fir tree. Keith offered his sisters' new rag dolls a ride in his own new wagon, and Jonathan and Mark went to help with the morning chores.

Sandy stirred the coals in the stove, and Pam dropped the first spoonfuls of pancake batter on the griddle. But the sizzling was soon drowned out by Joe's excited shouts. "Rachel! Rachel! Come down here and see who's turned up to spend the holidays with us!"

Pam and Sandy reached the door first, but Rachel shrieked from the head of the stairs and dashed down into the arms of a tall, slender stranger with dark curly hair and a full, black beard. "Aaron! Aaron, darling! What are you doing here? Can you stay?"

Joe, who had disappeared when Rachel came down, was back before Rachel had disentangled herself from the visitor. "Daniel, meet your Uncle Aaron." Joe smiled proudly as he handed the wide-eyed baby to the young man.

Rachel, still panting with excitement, turned to the growing audience behind her. "This is my kid brother, Aaron Levy. I haven't seen him in, oh, it must be five years now. He was still in high school when Joe and I moved to California."

"Welcome to the ranch," David grinned, holding out his hand to the beaming young man. "We're just about to have breakfast."

Over steaming pancakes, Aaron began to answer Rachel and Joe's eager questions. "I was just finishing my first year at rabbinical school when the comet hit. And with Mother and Father gone—" Rachel and Joe already knew Rachel's parents had died in one of the terrible fires. "Well, there just didn't seem to be much

point in studying right then. I just started bumming
around, doing what I could for people, heading west."

"I kept waiting for word." There was a touch of
rebuke in Rachel's voice. "I knew about Mother and
Father, but we didn't know if you were dead or alive."

"Yeah. I'm sorry, Rachel. But the postal service
wasn't working that well, and I really didn't know what
I was doing or where I was going. Like so many
others, I was in shock." Aaron looked around at the
warm kitchen and well-stocked table. "You people
seem to have made out fairly well."

"God has been good to us all," David told him.
"The Lord has given us protection and enough to eat."

"It is nothing short of miraculous the way we
were sent here, Aaron." Rachel tried to tell him everything at once. "We were burned out, and David and
Pam opened their home to us. Sandy, Pam's sister, was
widowed during the meteor shower, but she did a
wonderful job as midwife. Daniel was born the day
after the comet hit. We've been taken in and wel-
comed as members of the family."

"Then you've been spared the worst of it too?"

"Yes, Aaron." Rachel couldn't take her eyes off
her brother. "We've had shelter, food, and precious
friends. And you certainly look well."

"I've been blessed with a miracle or two myself."
Aaron smiled confidently. "Rachel, were the locusts
bad here?"

"Ooh, awful!" A shudder surged around the
breakfast table as everyone concurred. "We've all got a
few scars, but thank God they are gone now," Rachel
continued.

"I was never bitten," Aaron said.

David, sitting at the far end of the table, gasped. "You were never bitten?"

"No, never. There were quite a few of us who weren't, actually. A bunch of us were rounded up and sent to a hospital down in Arizona to be studied. The doctors never did figure it out, but several thousand young men—all Jewish, by the way—seemed to be unappetizing to the awful creatures. So I lived out most of the summer in comfort, at government expense."

Excited glances shot around the table as the Cristmans and their houseguests digested this startling information. "Funny we never heard anything about that on the news," David muttered. "All men, all young, all Jewish?"

"All men and all Jewish," Aaron confirmed. "A handful were middle-aged or older, but the vast majority were in their late teens and early twenties."

"They sent you to the hospital just to study you? You're sure there's nothing wrong?" asked Rachel.

"Absolutely nothing, Rachel. They were just trying to find out why we were immune, in hopes of finding something to help the rest of you . . . a vaccine or something like that. But, I guess, they never did figure it out."

"The locusts didn't bite at all? Or were you just immune to the venom?" David asked.

"Not bitten at all. They'd buzz around, would light on us sometimes, but then just fly off, as though we smelled bad." Aaron laughed, but a puzzled frown hovered between his eyes. "It was uncanny, as though they wanted to bite, but couldn't."

"So the 144,000 who were sealed really were young Jewish men—single, presumably celibate, Jewish men." David turned to Joe. "You know, I was a little surprised when you proved susceptible to the stings, but now I think I understand."

"What does he mean, Joe?"

"It's part of the prophecy, Aaron." Joe hesitated, doubtful about how his brother-in-law would react to his and Rachel's conversions. "The book of Revelation, part of the Christian New Testament, speaks of 144,000 Jewish men, undefiled by women, who would be sealed by God, protected from the locusts."

"Christian prophecies." Aaron shrugged. "The Christians have only false prophets."

There was a moment of awkward silence before Rachel spoke again. "Well, you're safe, and that's all I care about right now. We can talk about the rest later. You are going to stay here with us, aren't you?"

Aaron glanced quickly from his sister to their host. David saw the question in Aaron's eyes and agreed, "Sure, Aaron. We want you to stay on. The house is big, and we need all the help we can get with the farm work."

"Thanks, but I don't plan to stay long. I'm on my way to Jerusalem."

"Jerusalem!" Rachel gasped. "But Israel is a wasteland. They say there is nothing there anymore. Since the earthquakes a year ago there is virtually no Jerusalem left."

"Not exactly. The city may have been destroyed, but not the dream of our people. The rebuilding is already begun, and Secretary General Crosetti himself has guaranteed our safety. In a way, the destruction has been good. It has cleansed the Moslem desecration from the Holy Place."

"You mean the destruction of the Dome of the Rock, of course," Joe interrupted. "I have heard talk of the rebuilding of the temple."

"Yes, Joe. At the hospital I met a man—one of us. He has had a vision. Under his leadership, we will rebuild the temple and prepare the land."

"Prepare the land for what, Aaron?" Joe frowned slightly.

"For the Messiah's kingdom."

Now there was a general gasp from Aaron's attentive listeners, and he seemed to enjoy the effect his announcement was having on them. "Yes, we believe the Messiah, the true prophet of the Lord, is coming very soon. Moise, the man I spoke of, is his forerunner. We are going to Jerusalem to meet our King."

"I hope you will stay with us for a little while at least, Aaron. There are things we would like to talk to you about."

"Of course. That's one reason I came, Joe. But I hope you and Rachel will decide to come with me to Jerusalem."

Aaron did stay on for a couple of weeks. But he was obviously uncomfortable in the Cristman household. Joe and Rachel tried to explain their new beliefs to him, but Aaron fought the fact that his own sister could have become a Christian.

One cold morning, as they all lingered over breakfast, Aaron confronted his sister and her husband. "Christians worship other gods. You know there is only one true God."

"Yes, Aaron." Rachel breathed an instant prayer for the right words. "We know there is only one true God; but we believe, now, that Jesus was the human manifestation of God. We know Jesus was the promised Messiah, Aaron. And the Messiah was God, existing for a time in a human body."

"That's nonsense. God cannot be bottled up in a human body. God is eternal, universal, unknowable."

"Aaron, it is because he is unknowable that he became a man. He did that in order to reveal himself to us."

"My own sister, my only family, my Rachel. Mother dead, Father dead. Now my own sister dead also." Aaron pushed his chair back from the table. "I am going to pack. It is time for me to move on."

"No, Aaron. Don't leave like this. If you would only stay with us a little longer, study the prophecies. Aaron, if a prophet speaks as from God and his prophecies come true, then he is a prophet of God. Our Scriptures teach that." .

"Our Scriptures teach first, and foremost, that God is One. I simply cannot stay any longer under the same roof as those who worship this false messiah, Jesus. You will soon see; our true Messiah is coming soon. And then you will understand!"

"The Messiah is coming soon, Aaron. You're right about that," Joe said gently.

"But you say he has already come."

"He has come and has been rejected. But he

promised to come again and establish his eternal kingdom."

"I'm sorry, Joe. I always liked you, and Rachel is my own flesh and blood. But you have left the faith of our fathers. You are dead to me now, and lost to the kingdom. I came here hoping to take you and her with me to Jerusalem to be part of the glory." Aaron sighed heavily. "I wanted you to be part of the joy that we will have there. But I see I must go without you."

"Not yet. Please, Aaron, stay just a little longer," Rachel pleaded.

"No. There is no point in my staying on. I am going to Jerusalem with Moise to rebuild the temple. We will be there waiting when our Messiah, our true Messiah, comes to reign!"

14

Life was hard at the Cristman ranch that spring and summer, as it was everywhere, but at the ranch the hard work was rewarded. Cows calved, and in a few months there was tender baby beef to be canned. There were plenty of chickens for meat and eggs. The huge vegetable garden flourished, and Pam, with Sandy's and Rachel's help, refilled her pantry shelves.

In Little Valley, and all over the world, weary people cheered when a beaming Secretary Crosetti proclaimed that all the troubles were over.

"But why do we have to go back to school?" Mark protested when the news came that Little Valley's school system would reopen in September. "We did fine last year with Joe and Rachel teaching us."

"For one thing, Mark," Sandy explained, "Joe is going back to his regular teaching job. For another, you can learn things at a regular school that Joe and

Rachel aren't equipped to teach you—subjects they haven't studied, things we don't have books about here."

"But, Mom, if there are only four or five years at most until the Lord comes, what difference does it make? Besides," Jonathan argued, "Uncle Dave needs our help on the ranch, especially if Mr. Stenberg's going back to teaching."

It was hard for Sandy to fault Jonathan's logic. "We think there will only be four or five years, Jon, but we don't know for sure. So, young men, we each have to keep doing our jobs until he does come. And your job is to go to school."

Jonathan shrugged. "I guess it will be fun to hang out with some other kids for a change. At least it'll get my kid brother out of my hair." He punched Mark playfully.

"Same here. Mom, do you have any idea how he bosses me around?"

"It will be good for both of you to be on your own a little more."

"It will be good for them," Sandy repeated to Pam as they washed the dinner dishes. "But all the same, I'm glad they'll be going to and from town with Joe."

"*You're* glad?" Pam sighed. "Stephanie's only six years old. I don't care what Crosetti says about the world being back to normal. It isn't. I just pray that God will protect my little girl."

Pam paused. *Yes,* she mused, *Stephanie has become mine, hasn't she?*

*   *   *

All too soon, Pam and Sandy learned that the biggest danger to their children was not in the daily trip to town and back.

Stephanie had been delighted at the prospect of going to school, and she came home the first day bubbling over with excitement. "I learned lots of things in school already, Mommy."

"You did, Stephanie? What did you learn today?" Pam smiled as the little girl plopped down on a kitchen chair and gulped a glass of milk.

She swallowed, took a deep breath, and began to share her newly acquired knowledge. "I learned about Secretary General Crosetti being dead and coming back to life. He is a very great man, and our teacher says we should always do what he says."

Pam glanced at Sandy, who was making sandwiches for her always-hungry sons. "Stephanie," she said quickly, "we should always obey the laws, unless they tell us something different from what Jesus has told us."

"The secretary general wouldn't do that," Stephanie piped, wiping her milk mustache off with her arm. "Teacher says he loves Jesus. We have a picture in our room of him praying in front of a cross with Jesus on it."

"Stephanie, I want you to tell us every night what you learned in school that day." Pam's face was intense, serious.

"And that goes for you boys too," Sandy added, handing Jonathan and Mark their snacks.

*   *   *

Pam met the children at the kitchen door when they came home from school a couple of weeks later. Stephanie, as usual, reached for the milk and cookies Pam had ready, but Mark just shook his head.

"No, thanks, Aunt Pam," Jonathan echoed. "I'm really not hungry right now." Both boys brushed past her and headed upstairs.

"Are they mad at me, Mommy?"

"Why would they be mad at you?"

"I don't know, but Mark and Jon didn't say hardly anything all the way home, and neither did Mr. Stenberg."

The door slammed behind Joe. "Hello, Pam," he muttered. "Dave still digging potatoes?"

"As a matter of fact he came in a few minutes ago. He's upstairs, washing up. Joe, what's the matter?"

"Stephanie, would you go upstairs and tell your Daddy Dave to come down here, please?" Joe almost pushed the little girl through the door.

"Joe," Pam repeated. "What's wrong?"

David asked the same question from halfway down the staircase.

Joe slumped into a kitchen chair. "I guess there's not that big a hurry, but I brought some bad news. I didn't want to tell you in front of Stephanie."

"Didn't want to tell us *what* in front of her?" Sandy asked, coming in the back door with a basket of fresh eggs. "Is there trouble at school?"

"No. It has nothing to do with school, Sandy. Just sad news about some old friends."

"Who, Joe?" Pam urged.

"The Masters."

"Bill and Wilma?" David asked.

Joe nodded. "Pastor Frank told me this afternoon. He went out to their place yesterday. The place was overgrown. He couldn't rouse anybody."

"I haven't heard anything about them in town for quite a while. I knew Bill was having trouble farming that slope." David shook his head. "I guess I should have ridden over to see if I could help. Well, they probably moved on."

"They didn't move on, Dave."

"What do you mean, Joe? You said no one was there."

"Not exactly. The motor home was still there. Frank found them in it . . . the whole family . . . all dead."

It was Pam who finally broke the stunned silence. "How, Joe?"

"It had been quite a while. But as near as anyone can tell . . . well, each of them had been killed by a single shot in the head."

"But why?" David's voice quavered with pain. "Robbery?"

"Bill had a gun in his hand with four bullets missing."

"But if he were fighting off someone?" Pam didn't want to believe what Joe was implying.

"No, Pam. Bill shot his wife and children, apparently while they slept. And then killed himself."

"Oh, no . . . I wouldn't have thought that of Bill, Joe. He always seemed so tough," Pam said in a soft weak voice.

"And they were Christians too. How could he do such a horrible thing?" Sandy wondered.

"He left a note for Pastor Frank. He just gave up. Lost hope."

"Oh, no," Pam moaned. "Like Tom, but worse."

"So much worse." Sandy thought of her sons. "How could anyone kill his own children?"

"Frank found the note in Bill's Bible. He showed it to me." Joe bit his lip angrily. "Bill said in the note that God had deserted them, and all of us, and he couldn't go on alone. He said all the promises were lies. He said Frank had lied to him, and worse, God had lied to him."

It was several moments before Joe spoke again. "You know, I'm worried about Frank. He's taking this terribly hard, as if he were blaming himself for what happened."

"That's ridiculous."

"That's just what I told him, David. But he seems to think he should have had the answers, should have been able to explain what was happening."

"Frank's certainly not the only minister who taught a pretribulation Rapture." Sandy thought of Bob's certainties. "We're all confused."

"You know," Joe mused, "I think Rachel and I are the lucky ones. We never had all these expectations. No expectation, no disappointment."

David smiled at his friend. "You've actually been a help to me. Seeing the prophecies through your unprejudiced eyes has helped me realize the interpretations I'd learned weren't necessarily what the Word actually said."

"Yes, Joe," Pam agreed. "I've learned as much by answering your questions as I've taught you."

As was still their custom, the Cristman household drove David's team and wagon into Little Valley for church the next Sunday. Sometimes these ranchers constituted Frank's entire congregation.

"Doesn't anyone care about God anymore?" Pam wondered aloud, as she and David joined Peggy Braden. "Usually it's us, Frank, and you, Peggy. Sometimes Art comes, with Tammy. Nobody else. Wouldn't you think people would come to pray for mercy in times like these?"

"Maybe they think it's too late for mercy." Peggy shuffled uneasily. "I wouldn't be here if Tom knew. He thinks I work all day Sunday, but sometimes I can get someone to cover for me."

"It doesn't surprise me that most people either blame God for the troubles or deny his existence because of them," David commented. "But I find it hard to understand about Tom. He was an elder, one of our most faithful members, a soul winner."

"He still feels the same as he did last fall, when he tried to take his life. He thinks God went back on his Word. Maybe that was what happened with Bill Masters too."

"Wasn't that terrible, Peggy?" Pam shivered. "I still can't imagine anyone deliberately shooting his own children."

Peggy studied the dry grass at her feet. "I don't know. Sometimes I agree with Tom that God let us believe a lie."

THE REVELATION

"But now, in hindsight, Peggy, we can see we were trusting in man's ideas. The Rapture of the church was never that clearly spelled out. We were wrong. That doesn't mean God lied."

"Most of the time I see that, David. That's why I still come. I listen to Frank's sermons on God's sovereignty, and I can hold on to that again, for a few days. But I can understand the others too."

"I can't." Sandy had been talking with Frank, but now the two of them joined the Cristmans and Peggy. "I can't see how anyone can deny the Scriptures after all that's happened. How can anyone not see that these events are supernatural?"

Peggy shook her head. "Lots of them do see that, Sandy. That's the worst of it."

"She's right," Frank agreed. "Sandy, you're somewhat isolated out at the ranch. Well, we—David and I—agreed there was no need to worry you or Pam about this, but a lot of people in this town have found a new god. They say our Lord has lost the war, and Satan is in charge now."

Pam shuddered, and Sandy gulped in horror. "But, Frank, no one could worship Satan, no one in his right mind!"

"They do, Sandy. We have to worship something. God made us that way. If we reject God long enough—"

"I can't believe this," Sandy insisted. "I mean, there've always been little, isolated cults, but the fact that substantial numbers of people would openly worship the devil . . . I can't accept it. Tom isn't involved in that, is he, Peggy?"

"Not Tom, thank God. But have any of you talked to Helen Just lately?"

"Helen!" It was Pam's turn to gasp.

Frank glanced at his watch. "Unbelievable as it is, satanism is becoming more and more a common and accepted religion. But we do know the true God," he reminded them. "Shall we round up the children and begin our worship service?"

This handful of faithful ones sat in the salvaged pews under a makeshift roof. Frank accompanied them on his guitar as they sang a few familiar hymns.

He did not mention the Masters' tragedy. Instead, elaborating on his earlier words, Frank preached from 2 Thessalonians 2:10–11. "'. . . They did not receive the love of the truth, that they might be saved. And for this reason God will send them strong delusion, that they should believe the lie.'"

As Frank picked up his guitar to introduce the closing hymn, the worshipers heard harsh voices. Looking around, they realized they were encircled by about two dozen men and women dressed in tight-fitting black pants and T-shirts. Each wore a black, stocking mask. One, taller than the others, with an athletic build, strode between the pews.

"Preacher," he demanded. "Let's just see what's a lie and what's the truth. I say my god has already beaten your God, and I'll prove it by taking you on right here and now."

Frank stepped from the pulpit.

"Frank, don't be foolish," Sandy screamed. "Fighting him wouldn't prove—"

Frank lifted his hand and motioned for silence.

The hand shook, but Frank's voice never faltered. "The Lord will fight for us," he paraphrased Moses, "and we will hold our peace."

"Hear that?" the devilish leader sneered. "The old man is afraid to fight."

His masked followers jeered. "Go on, Preacher. If you worship the true God, prove it."

David stood, turned, and faced the enemy. "Get out of here, punk. We don't have to prove anything to you."

"Oh, look. He knows his God can't protect the preacher so he's going to do it for him."

The black-clad figures laughed and moved in closer to watch the brawl. But Frank pushed David aside and faced his adversary. "Mr. Cristman is right. We need prove nothing to you or to your father, the devil." Frank stood his ground, inches from the other man's clenched fist.

"Please," Sandy begged. "Go away and leave the pastor alone."

"The lady's asking us to go away, Preacher. Are you going to beg us to leave too?"

Pam shielded the three toddlers with her arms. Mark and Jonathan moved closer to their mother. Raucous laughter echoed across the circle of satanists.

"No, I am not going to beg you to leave." Frank seemed to grow taller as he looked up into the eyes that peered from within the mask. "I am telling you to leave. In the name of the Lord Jesus Christ, I command you to leave."

There wasn't a sound. The circle widened, each dark figure backed slowly from the ruins of the little church. The startled leader retreated, muttering, "We'll get you next time."

Shaken, the tiny congregation disbanded. "I'll walk you home, Peggy," Joe offered.

"Thank you, but I'm headed back to work at the hospital."

"Then I'll walk you there. You shouldn't go alone."

"All right, Joe. I guess I would appreciate the company."

Of those who formed a protective huddle around their pastor, Sandy stood closest. "You're coming back to the ranch with us, Frank. You can't stay here. You heard his threats."

"Yes, Frank," David agreed, "you'd better come home with us, for a few days at least."

"No, Sandy, Dave. I can't run. That's what they want me to do. Besides," he smiled, "I don't have to."

"But he said they'd be back. God only knows what they'll do."

"Obviously God is the only one who needs to know."

15

David guided the two straining horses across the billowy white meadow. Joe and Jonathan followed, bundling the cut buckwheat into loose, clumsy sheaves.

"Hey, Dave, look. Isn't that a car coming up the road?" Joe called. "It looks like Pastor Thomsen's Chevy."

"Sure does, Joe. It must be something important to bring him way out here on a Saturday when he'll see us tomorrow at church anyway. Let's find out what's up."

As the men started toward the house, the great Chinese gong on the porch rang furiously. They broke into a run, but the gong continued to clang until Rachel spied them from the porch. She was as breathless as they when the two men leaped the steps, two at a time. "It's Frank," she gasped. "They beat him up and burned his house."

"Who? Those hooded punks?" David demanded.

"Is he okay?" Joe asked.

Frank sat hunched over the kitchen table, his bloody shirt in a heap on the floor. He groaned as Sandy sponged the jaggedly torn skin of his pale back. He had been whipped.

"Frank!" David looked away from the ugly stripes and sat opposite his pastor. "Frank, who did this to you?"

Frank winced as he lifted his head, showing blackened eyes and bruised jaw. "Just those punks in stocking masks."

"The satanists," Rachel breathed, eyes wide with fear. "They said they'd get him."

"How dare they! How dare they walk around in that witch's garb and openly admit to worshiping the devil!" Sandy's touch remained soft, though her words were harsh. "And to attack the kindest, gentlest man in Little Valley."

"And their worst enemy. Frank's probably the only one who has had the courage to call their bluff."

"We know what drives people to such evil," Frank said. "Their father, the devil."

"I guess it's no different than it's always been, except that they openly admit it now." Frank glanced at the two women and then at his ruined shirt. "Dave, would you have a clean shirt I could borrow?"

"Jon, please run out and get something off the clothesline," Sandy said. "And, Frank, I'm going to get you a glass of milk and some fresh baked bread. Then I think you should lie down and try to get some rest."

"Yes, ma'am," Frank nodded.

But Pam had just come down from settling Beth and little Daniel for their naps and had more questions. "How did you get away, Frank? Why didn't they take your car?"

"That's really funny." He frowned, puzzled.

"I don't see anything funny about it," David muttered.

"Strange," Frank explained. "David, the starter on that car was shot. I haven't been able to get it running without a push for weeks."

"Thank God it worked this time," Sandy gasped.

David nodded. "Frank, Rachel said something about a fire. Do you feel up to telling us just what did happen?"

"I'd walked over to see Art and Helen. She's still awfully bitter, and he's so pitifully confused. Anyhow, I try to see them every few days to do what I can."

Sandy slipped the shirt, which Jonathan had brought, over Frank's bruised and lacerated shoulders. Frank continued: "When I got back, there were half a dozen of these satanists in my den, tearing up my books. One of them had my Bible in his hand. I asked him how he dared touch the Word of God, and he laughed." Frank shivered. "I swear it was a demonic laugh. I tried to take the Bible away from him, and that's when they jumped on me. Mostly they used their fists. One of them took my belt and used it on my back." He winced again. "Remember that western buckle I was always so proud of?"

It was Sandy's turn to wince at Frank's horrible story. "Then they set fire to the papers and torn books. They just stood there watching the books burn. I think they intended to leave me there to burn in the fire."

"How did you get away?" Pam asked gently.

"I crawled through the door to the garage, and, I don't know how, but I found I had the car key in my hand. I got in and turned it, and the car started. I just backed out right through the door and took off." He shook his head, then, in wonder. "That starter. It hasn't worked in weeks."

"It's dead now too," Joe announced. "I just went out to move the car around behind the barn, and it didn't even turn over."

Obviously Frank could not go home. So a cot was set up in the dining room, and he joined the growing community at the ranch.

Pam peered at her watch in the waning light the following Wednesday afternoon. "David, I knew we should keep the children home from school. They're late."

"They're not late, Pam. Joe was going to stop at Frank's place after school and see what he could salvage, remember?"

"But it's almost dark."

"Pam, don't worry," David tried to reassure her. "What happened to Frank was probably an isolated incident. They haven't hurt any children."

"Yet. As far as we know. I still think we should keep Stephanie home."

"Well, tomorrow's Thanksgiving, so we have a long weekend to think about it."

"She's so little and helpless."

"But Joe's reliable, darling. He'd tell us if there was anything to be afraid of."

David's consoling words were quickly confirmed by the sound of horses' hooves; in a moment Stephanie and the boys burst through the door. Pam hugged Stephanie even more closely than usual. "Did you have a good time at school today, honey?" She pulled the little girl onto her lap. "Tell Mommy all about it."

"We learned something about God in school today," Stephanie answered. "We learned he has lots of other names."

"What do you mean? Names like Jesus and Emmanuel and Christ?"

"No, Mommy. Names I never heard before. Teacher says God is called lots of things in other countries, but he's always the same God."

Pam probed further. "In other languages? What other names did she tell you God has, Stephanie?"

"Allah and Buddha and Vish . . . Vish something. I don't remember all of them."

David joined in: "Are you sure she said those were other names for God? Or did she say they were other gods?"

"Other names, Daddy David. She said Secretary General Crosetti and Brother Stan say there is only one God, and everybody worships him, but in different ways and by different names."

"Stephanie, listen to me, honey." David spoke softly but deliberately, trying to stifle his anger. "Stephanie, all those names are names of false gods. They are not the same as our God, or as Jesus. They

THE REVELATION

are idols, and you must never, never think of them as God. Do you understand?"

The little girl sensed the anger in his voice, and her eyes grew wide with fear. "But Daddy David, you said I should obey my teacher and the secretary general"

"Not when they tell you anything against God."

When Joe walked into the kitchen, Pam said, "Joe, what's going on in the schools? Are our children blatantly being taught idolatry?"

He nodded slowly. "I'm lucky, Pam. I teach chemistry. But there is pressure. It isn't like it was before, when any mention of religion was taboo. Now religion is in, but it's—" Joe spat out the name—"it's Crosetti's religion. He hasn't rewritten the chemistry texts, but literature, history. I don't know exactly what's happening in the grade schools, but I suspect Stephanie's report is pretty accurate."

"David," Pam said, "that settles it. If this is what is being taught—"

Mark interrupted. "Aunt Pam, we're getting pretty much the same thing in junior high. I didn't say anything because I knew you'd be upset, but almost all the teachers say it doesn't really matter what you believe as long as you believe something."

"Well, if that's true, I'm keeping Stephanie home and teaching her here."

"Us too?"

"Yes, Mark," Sandy agreed. "If you are being taught that, you and Jon can stay home too. Pam and Rachel and I will teach you, like we did last year."

After supper Sandy slipped into the darkened living room where Frank sat alone.

"Frank," she said softly, "why don't you turn on the light? Or, better yet, come join us in the kitchen. It's warmer there."

"Oh, Sandy." He started at the sound of her voice. "Oh, I was just sitting here thinking."

"About what happened?"

"About Thanksgiving, Sandy."

"We were, too, Frank. Come on. The family circle needs you."

Frank winced as he stood, but he smiled as he walked into the fire-lit kitchen. *Yes, a family circle,* he thought as he surveyed the household.

Pam and David were an ideal couple, if there could ever be such a thing. The only flaw in their marriage had been their inability to have children. But the three Turner youngsters had become as much theirs as if they had been born to them.

Mark and Jonathan sprawled in front of the stove, playing checkers by the glow of the fire. Sandy pulled a chair close to them and picked up her knitting. In one corner, Joe laughed as Rachel recounted Daniel's latest misadventures.

Suddenly Frank spoke. "Have you people any idea how much you have to be thankful for?"

"Yes, Frank, I think we know," Sandy responded. "And most of all, right now we're thankful you're here with us." She patted the chair next to hers. "Come here and sit down."

Frank carefully edged onto the kitchen chair, sparing himself the touch of its wooden back on his still raw flesh. "I'm thankful to be alive," he sighed, "but I keep wondering why... why did God do a miracle to spare my worthless life?"

"Obviously not worthless to him, Frank, and not to us either," Pam protested.

"Certainly not," David agreed.

"How can you even think such a thing, Frank?" Sandy demanded. "Why, without you, without your encouragement, we'd never have made it through the past two years."

"I hope I've been some help, to someone. I've failed so many."

"Frank!"

"No, Sandy, I have. I failed Tom. He's rejected God because I can't give him the answers he needs. The Justs—I can't reach Helen at all, and Art keeps asking why. And I can't tell him why."

"You've told us how, though, Frank. You've shown us how to keep going, how to keep trusting."

If Frank heard Sandy's words he ignored them. "Bill Masters. My God, why couldn't I help Bill?"

Sandy watched the firelight reflected in Frank's tear-filled eyes. "If they had only listened to you and trusted the Lord."

"Thank you, Sandy, but I know I failed them. God knows I tried, but so much of the time I was mouthing the words. If only I had learned sooner."

He sighed deeply and dropped his chin into his cupped palms. "Sandy, all of you—" Frank's gaze moved slowly around the room. "I couldn't convince Bill or Tom or the Justs or so many others, because of my own doubts."

"No, Frank," Sandy protested. "That isn't true. You've been our strength."

"Yes, Frank." Pam, too, sensed Frank's despair. "Your sermons on the endurance of Job have inspired us all to hold on."

"I wasn't preaching the book of Job, Pam. I was living it, with all the doubts and all the self-justification."

"We knew, Frank." David broke in. "We all drew strength from your patience."

"Patience!" Frank snorted. "I always did think Job was one of the least patient people who ever lived. He did nothing but complain. He argued with God for thirty-one chapters. He was no better than his friends."

"That's an interesting shift in interpretation."

"Scholars misinterpreted a lot of other scripture, too, Dave. Why not Job?"

"But there was one difference, Frank, between Job and his friends."

"Yes." Frank smiled then. "There was one important difference. Job argued with God, but he never denied him. He didn't understand, but he trusted."

"It was easier to trust when we thought we understood, Frank. These past two years we've all had our doubts."

"I wasn't supposed to, David. I was the pastor. I was supposed to have the answers, or at least I thought I was supposed to have them."

"Oh, Frank." Sandy tried to soothe him. "You gave us the only answer that mattered. You taught us to trust God in spite of everything. You helped us to hang on, to keep faith."

"It took me so long, Sandy. I struggled for the answers for two years. Now I realize I don't need to know, only to trust. I said Job's words so many times they finally sunk in. But maybe—if I'd been speaking from my heart instead of to it—maybe I could have helped the others."

"You had more faith than all the rest of us put together, Frank." Sandy covered his trembling hand with her own. "Why, when the satanists came to the church you had the faith to order them away in the name of Christ."

"Oh, no, Sandy. I was still full of doubt even then."

He saw their astonishment and continued. "When I commanded them in Christ's name to go away, I was almost as surprised as they were. I knew in my mind that my God was true and would honor his Word, but in my heart I still doubted."

"But you still did it," Sandy reminded him.

"What else could I do? But even then I wasn't convinced, down deep. I rationalized. I figured they were bluffing and I'd call their bluff too. But then they came back."

A chill swept the room; everyone listening shivered as Frank continued his confession. "I was sure I was going to die, and all I could think of was that over-worked text from Job: 'Though He slay me, yet will I trust Him.'"

He gazed around the circle again. "And here I am."

"Amen. Praise the Lord."

"Amen. Dave. And because I am here I know, at

last, that there is still a God in charge of this mad, mad world; and I know I am in his care."

Sandy finally spoke for them all. "Thank you, Frank. Your encouragement through the dark times means even more to us now, knowing that you were struggling with doubt, just as we were."

"Thank God for the assurance of his care for all of us." David bowed his head. "What more do we need?"

CHAPTER

16

The mountains above Little Valley received a surprise dusting of snow the night before Christmas, and the ranch, for the moment, was a Christmas card image of peace. David had cut a small fir tree, and Pam took the old ornaments from the box in the attic to trim it.

Beth, Stephanie, and Keith were up before dawn. They scrambled for the stockings they had hung behind the wood stove; they squealed with delight over the chestnuts and homemade cookies Pam had stuffed into them.

Frank had carved a jointed wooden doll for each of the girls, and David and Joe had made rocking cradles for them. Daniel nibbled at the ear of his stuffed puppy for a few minutes before burrowing into its reused tissue wrappings.

Mark and Jonathan found new, hand-knit turtleneck sweaters under the little tree and gave their

THE REVELATION

mother a thank-you hug before bundling up to go help David with the milking.

Then Jonathan came back in, setting the brimming milk pails on the kitchen counter, and peeking past his mother, who stooped over the plump turkey in the oven. "Mmmm. That looks good, Mom. When do we eat?"

"Don't be silly. It looks raw, which it is! Breakfast will be ready in about ten minutes though." Sandy straightened up and started to give her son a maternal pat and send him upstairs to wash. But suddenly she realized she was facing a young man who grinned at her at eye level. Instead, she said, "You've just got time to get cleaned up."

As Jonathan vanished, Sandy turned to her sister, who was beating eggs for an omelet. "When did he grow up, Pam?"

"I was wondering that myself a couple of weeks ago. When you first came here he was a little boy."

"And now he's as tall as I am. Why, Pam, he's almost fifteen. Where has the time gone?"

"It's been over two years."

"Two years already. It's gone so fast; so much has happened, things we never dreamed we'd see."

"Like what?" Frank entered the kitchen and sniffed the homey smells of toast and coffee. "Breakfast?"

Sandy laughed along with him. "Ten minutes. You're as bad as Jon."

"And what's Jon been up to now?"

"Nothing." Pam slipped the omelet pan into the

oven. "We were just talking about how much he's grown up in the past two years."

"That wasn't one of the things you never expected to see, I hope." Frank took the coffeepot from Sandy and set it on the breakfast table.

"No. Both of my sons' health and maturity are the good things." Sandy gazed past Frank to the pure white world outside the kitchen window. "So many sad things—the destruction, the misery. I was always so sure we would never see the Tribulation. Bob was sure too . . . like Bill . . . like Tom."

Sandy stood quiet for a few moments. "I miss him so sometimes." Her lonely eyes seemed drawn to Frank's as she continued flatly. "I'm glad he's gone. I'm glad he's with the Lord and not here amid this pain and confusion. Does that sound terrible?"

Pam reached out to touch her sister's clenched hand, but Frank reached it first and held it gently in his own. "Is it wrong for me to thank God that Anne, too, was spared all this?"

The silence among the three of them was answer enough.

The Christmas turkey was roasted on schedule, and at dinner time the long, pine table was laden with the ranch's finest fruits and vegetables. There was homemade cornbread from home-ground meal, golden squash generously buttered, a crisp apple-and-walnut salad. Everyone feasted happily and gratefully.

Then, just as Pam and Sandy passed warm slices of apple pie, someone began rapping furiously on the front door. "Stay here," David ordered, suddenly sober. No one had to be told twice. "Oh, no," they heard

David say as he opened the door. "Oh, no, Art, what's happened?"

Chairs scraped in the kitchen, but David called out again, "It's all right. It's Art Just and Tammy. We'll be there in a minute."

Art carried his granddaughter in, but his shoulders sagged under the light load. Dark circles under his sunken eyes, sharply protruding cheekbones, loose flesh along the line of his once-firm jaw seemed to add decades to his age. David took the child from his arms.

"Had to get Tammy out here to you," Art stammered, lurching toward a padded Boston rocker. "Had to bring Tammy here. Knew she'd be safe here."

"What do you mean, Art? Why is Tammy in danger?"

Frank now stood nearby, shocked by his old friend's haggard appearance. "Keep the kids out here," he whispered to Pam, as David handed a strangely silent Tammy to him. "And give this tyke some dinner." He put Tammy in Pam's outstretched arms and followed David back into the living room.

"Art, how did you get here?" Frank knew the Justs had sold the Buick months ago for grocery money. "And where is Helen?"

"Walked. Walked all the way. Had to get here without Helen knowing."

David and Frank exchanged worried glances. "Why didn't you want Helen to know?" Frank feared Art's mind had failed completely now. "Won't Helen worry if you and Tammy are missing?"

"Helen doesn't worry anymore. Helen has all the

answers now." Art spoke flatly. "I had to get Tammy away from her. Helen wants to kill her."

"Kill her!" Frank gasped. "Art, you don't mean that. Helen adores Tammy. She'd never hurt her."

"Helen—" Art gripped the arms of the chair as he slumped further into it. "Helen isn't herself."

"We know Helen has been disturbed. She's had so much grief in such a short time, Art. But she'd never hurt Tammy."

"Do you believe in witches, Pastor?"

Frank wanted to comfort the old man, but casual words would do no good now. "The Bible says as much about demons as about angels."

"Helen is possessed, Frank. I'm sure of it."

"Helen is grief-stricken, Art," David protested. "But how could you think she's demon-possessed?"

"She goes to their meetings, the satanists' meetings."

"So Peggy was right," David recalled her words about Helen on the Sunday the satanists first threatened Frank.

"Now, Art, you can't be sure of that," Frank remonstrated.

"She does," he insisted. "It all started after the comet, after Jimmy. She managed to accept the other deaths, but Jimmy was different. You remember how she went to the grave and just sat there for days. She came home, but she kept talking to him. A woman told her he wasn't dead."

"But we know that, Art. He's with the Lord."

"That's not what she meant, Pastor Frank. She talked Helen into a séance. Helen believes she has seen Jimmy, and Paul and Terry too. This woman called up their spirits."

David shuddered. Frank persisted in his gentle prodding. "Art, people can be deceived, especially in times like these. Helen was so hurt. I'll go and talk to her."

"No! Pastor, stay away from her." The voice was tired, but it was not the voice of a crazy old man. Art spoke from sincere, intense terror.

"Pastor Frank, she's involved with the satanists. No, not just involved. She's one of them. She goes to all the meetings." His haunted eyes searched his friends' faces. "You don't want to believe it, do you? Well, I didn't either, not for a long time. But she goes out late at night, and the next morning there's food in the house."

"That doesn't mean—" Frank interrupted, but Art persisted.

"Every time she's out at night I hear later that someone else has been attacked and robbed. I found a box of jewelry yesterday morning. I recognized some of it. It belonged to our friends in town, friends who have been robbed by the satanists."

"Art, even if Helen has been driven to crime by her pain, I can't believe she would hurt Tammy."

"I followed her last night. I listened outside."

Joe and the women had gathered, silent, in the doorway, as Art reluctantly continued. "I listened, and they were talking about Christmas. One of them muttered something about needing a sacrifice, an atonement. They dared to use that word—an *atonement* for their father. He said, 'God sent a child.' That's what their leader said. 'God sent a child, and we must offer a child too.'"

"A child? No, Art, you can't believe that."

"Yes, I do, Frank. And you do too. You don't want to believe it, but you do. They intend to sacrifice a child to Satan. The leader specifically asked Helen to provide the sacrifice, and she agreed! My Helen agreed . . . my Helen . . ."

An icy wind chilled the ranch house which moments ago had been so warm with the joy of Christmas. Now, everyone shivered as Art lifted his gaunt face to them. "I had to bring Tammy to you. You will let her stay here, won't you? She'll be safe here, with your armed guards. Please, you must protect her!"

David glanced at Pam, who nodded wordlessly. "Of course, Tammy can stay with us, Art. You both can. But why here, Art? Why did you feel she would be safe here? We have no armed guards."

Art looked bewildered. "You know, the soldiers camped out in your pasture."

Art looked from face to puzzled face. "You don't know, do you? You really don't know."

"Art, there are no soldiers camped in our pasture or anywhere around here. We work in those fields and in the woods. We'd know if there were an encampment in the neighborhood."

"But in town—" Art stammered, fear returning to his face. "But Helen told me herself, and some men in town were talking about it too."

"Talking about what, Art?"

"About this ranch. Well, about some ranch out

this way that had plenty of food and horses. Who else has plenty of food and horses?"

David felt almost guilty as he looked around the cozy, Christmasy room.

Art shrugged and continued. "Anyhow, several gangs had gone out to rob it; but every time they tried, when they got to the edge of the pasture, they saw these soldiers, all in white uniforms. The white soldiers surrounded the place. So nobody dared to go any closer. It sure sounded like your place, Dave."

Only a child could have spoken then, and it was Mark's childlike faith that immediately posed the question: "Angels! Pastor Frank, do you think angels are protecting us?"

"Maybe so, son. Maybe so."

"I've heard of such miraculous things, on the mission field, places like that. But we're just ordinary people," David mused. "Would God really send his angels just to protect our ranch?"

"It is uncanny, David, that most of our neighbors have been robbed, yet we haven't been touched." Frank remembered finding the car key in his hand the day he was beaten. "He has done other miracles for us. Maybe he has sent his angels too."

"We've been taking his protection for granted sometimes, haven't we?" Sandy spoke for them all. "There is an angel army guarding us, whether we or anyone else can see them or not. The Lord promised he would preserve us, and we all know he has."

Art did share their thanksgiving prayer, and their Christmas dinner spread abundantly on the festive trestle table. But he refused their invitation to stay on.

"No, I have an obligation to Helen." He sighed a sigh that shook his whole body. "She is my wife. Just take care of Tammy. Please, take care of Tammy."

Perhaps the Cristman household's unwillingness to fully believe Art's words about the satanic sacrifice prevented their pressing him to stay with them. Perhaps it was a subconscious fear that the evil which clung so close to him might sneak into their place of peace. Perhaps the satanic events were inevitable, just one more expression of God's judgment. Whatever the case, each of the people at the ranch would wonder, too late, if they could have done anything to prevent the tragedy that followed.

The next morning, in the redwood grove behind the Little Valley Church, Art Just's body was found, riddled with knife wounds . . . the satanic symbol of the inverted, five-pointed star cut deeply into the flesh of his forehead, a symbol of the hatred and religious perversion that was ravaging the earth and Little Valley.

17

Art Just's horrible death and Helen's subsequent disappearance rocked Little Valley almost as much as the earthquakes of the past two years. Even the most cynical of the townspeople had to accept the sinister, supernatural circumstances surrounding them. And so the satanists were forced back into hiding.

The same law that had been so slow to curb the satanists was quick, however, to enforce the truancy regulations. Soon after the end of Christmas vacation, the authorities determined that the Cristman's wards and the Peters' boys were deliberately being kept out of school. Late in January a court order was delivered to the ranch by two sheriff's deputies.

"I'm awfully sorry, David." One of the two deputies, who was an old friend, stood dutifully before David with the order. "I sure hate to be the one to do this."

David took the document and read it quickly.

"What is it, David?" Pam asked.

David slowly reread the single page. "But this just can't be. I don't believe it."

"What, David?" Pam tried to take the paper, but David held it out just out of her reach. "It's some sort of mistake, Pam. Just some stupid, bureaucratic mistake."

"I wish it were, Dave, but it's a binding court order. We have to take Stephanie, Keith, and Elizabeth Turner from your custody and deliver them to juvenile hall immediately."

The deputy forced himself to look at Pam. "Mrs. Cristman, would you like to pack some things for the children? We'll let you have a few minutes to say good-bye."

"Good-bye? Juvenile hall?" Pam's breath came in short, heavy gasps. "Why? David, you've got to tell me. What's in that paper?"

David pulled her into the circle of his outstretched arm. "Pam, darling, the authorities have decided we are unfit parents to Stephanie because we refused to send her to school. And of course, once they started to investigate, they found we had three children here who were, technically, not ours."

"But they have no one else. We've cared for them for almost two years."

"Then why didn't you file for legal custody, ma'am?" The second deputy spoke roughly.

"With who?" David demanded. "We brought those children here the day before the comet struck. The world was in chaos. Who was worrying about legal custody when thousands of people were dying?" He shouted at the deputies as he cradled a sobbing Pam in his arms.

Their deputy friend stared at the ground, but his partner rasped. "As you said yourself, that was almost two years ago. Secretary Crosetti reestablished pre-existing legal structures over a year ago. You've had ample time to follow the proper procedures. Instead, you flaunted the law. You refused to file the proper custody papers, and you refused to send a school-age child to school."

"That's ridiculous!" David insisted. "The custody filing is nothing but a technicality. We can take care of that immediately. Surely we can keep the children here while the papers are being processed."

Pam lifted her head from David's shoulder. "We can go to the county seat with them right now."

"David, Mrs. Cristman, I'm sorry, but it would be too late by the time we got back. The offices would be closed."

"We're wasting time here," the second deputy snarled. "Come on, we've got our orders. Pack up the kids' stuff and get them out here."

Pam looked helplessly at David, who appealed once more to his old friend. "You know us. Can't you let us bring them in tomorrow and straighten this thing out?"

"I'd give anything if I could. Really I would. But you do have the children here illegally, and you have refused to send the girl to school. The judge had no choice." He shrugged. "And neither do we."

"But there must be some recourse," David pleaded. "Surely no one wants these children sent to juvenile hall, especially when they have a good, loving home here. We're teaching them. We can prove that. Rachel Stenberg is teaching them. She's an accredited teacher and so is her husband, Joe."

"Of course you can petition the court for custody, David," their friend advised. "But unless you settle the school question, you aren't likely to get it." As his partner half-followed, half-pushed David and Pam up the porch steps, he turned to Sandy, who watched in horror. "And be careful, Mrs. Peters. You could lose your boys too."

Three, small, bewildered faces stared from the window of the sheriff's car as it rolled down the drive. As they trudged back into the suddenly silent house, David's arms tensed around Pam. "Where is our angel army now, Lord?" she sobbed.

"Thank God her father's parents were able to take Tammy," David reminded her. "At least she's safe. Not only from the satanists but from the county too!"

No one ate much supper that night, but they lingered together around the kitchen table. "If we have to send Stephanie back to school, David, it would still be better than losing the kids entirely. We'd still be able to teach them the Lord's Word here."

"Yes," Sandy agreed, frightened by the deputy's parting words about her own sons.

"We'll be all right, Mom," Mark assured her. "Mr. Stenberg's with us going and coming, and the police have the satanists scared off anyhow."

"It doesn't matter that much what our teachers say," Jonathan offered. "Mark and I are old enough to know what's true and what's propaganda."

"But Stephanie isn't." Pam's voice still quivered, and she was hoarse from crying. "We can't just let the government take them, David."

"No," he agreed, looking at her swollen, tear-stained face. "No. Anything would be better than that."

Jonathan and Mark returned to school the next morning, and Pam and David were optimistic as they drove to the county seat. But they soon found their bureaucratic struggle had only begun.

"The children almost certainly have living relatives," the social worker stated coldly. "We can hardly award you custody without their consent."

"But we don't know if there is anyone, or who or where they are."

"They can be found, Mr. Cristman. There are copies of birth records in Sacramento, and families can still be traced, in spite of the events of the past two years."

"But what about temporary custody?" Pam pleaded.

"You can file an application." The officious woman pulled a thick form from her desk drawer. "But in light of your irresponsible actions, I doubt you would be considered suitable foster parents."

"Irresponsible actions! If you mean pulling innocent children out—"

"David," Pam interrupted him and spoke to the social worker. "Mrs. Sullivan, Mr. Cristman, and I have agreed that Stephanie can return to school. Please, just let the children come back to us. They need us."

The custody application was soon fed into the bureaucratic labyrinth that even the Great Tribulation had not succeeded in destroying, and for weeks it bounced from desk to desk.

Pam and David were permitted to visit the three children once at juvenile hall. Keith and Stephanie seemed to have adjusted fairly well. "We have to go to school here, and they tell us different things than you did, or Mommy and Daddy," Keith explained. "But we believe in Jesus, and we recite our Bible verses and say our prayers every day."

"Good for you," David encouraged. "We pray for you every day too."

But little Beth clung to Pam when the time came for them to part. "I want my Mommy Pam," she cried. "My other Daddy went away, and my other Mommy went away. Don't go away and leave me here, Mommy Pam. I want to go home with you."

"I want to take you with me, darling. Oh, how I want to take you with me. But I can't, Beth. Not yet."

In March, word came that the preliminary custody hearing was set for early May. But with it came word that the children had a surviving great-grandmother in Eureka. David and Pam used the whole month's ration of gas to drive up to see her.

"I love my granddaughter's children," she told them, wiping the tears from her cheeks. "But I can't possibly care for them." They followed her glance around the canvas-roofed shelter she shared with three other elderly women.

"You were friends of their parents, and you obviously love the children. Can't you keep them, even adopt them?"

"We want to, very much," David explained. "We have applied for custody, but the laws are complicated. If you would just appear at the hearing?"

"How could I? I can't travel that far at my age under today's conditions." The old lady sighed. "I want to help. Would a letter help?"

Pam and David knew that their prayers, and the prayers of all the Christians in Little Valley, were with them the day of the hearing. But the thought of the three young lives being entrusted to someone else, someone who might not teach them to fear the Lord, weighed heavily on their hearts.

The judge was very businesslike. He studied the application before him and questioned the same cold social worker Pam and David had seen before. "I think under the circumstances, the failure to file for custody can be considered irrelevant. The real issue, as I see it, is the children's education. Do you agree, Mrs. Sullivan?"

"Yes, Your Honor. The petitioners removed the oldest child from school because of a disagreement with the public policy on the teaching of religion in the schools."

The judge's hard look softened as he turned to David. "What provisions do you intend to make for the children's education if I should grant you temporary custody, Mr. Cristman?"

David sighed, but Pam squeezed his hand sharply.

"We will send the children to school as required by law, Your Honor," Pam promised.

The social worker interrupted. "There is a grandmother, Your Honor."

"A great-grandmother, Mrs. Sullivan. I know." He turned to Pam, who was glad to see the judge was smiling. "I received, this morning, a duly notarized statement from the children's great-grandmother who appears to be their only living relative. She states that she has talked to the Cristmans, that she shares their beliefs and feels they coincide with those of the children's deceased parents. She also states that she is physically unable to care for the children. In view of her statement, and other character references in my possession, I find no reason to deny this petition."

"Thank you, Lord," Pam whispered. "Thank you."

The judge rapped his gavel. "The bailiff will proceed to remand custody of Stephanie, Keith, and Elizabeth Turner to David and Pamela Cristman."

Pam and David hugged each other ecstatically. "They're ours, David." Pam sobbed with joy. "Praise the Lord, the children are ours."

The judge raised his voice. "Mr. and Mrs. Cristman, I must remind you that I have only granted temporary custody. You may petition for permanent custody in due course; but in the meantime, the children remain with you under court supervision and at the sufferance of the court."

"Mommy?" Keith tugged at her skirt as Pam straightened up.

"Shhh, Keith. Beth is finally asleep." She bent again to hear the little boy's whisper.

"Mommy, if the social welfare lady comes and takes us away again, you and Daddy David will come and find us, won't you, like Jesus found the lost sheep?"

"Keith, the lady won't take you away again. The judge said you could stay with us now."

"But if she does, you will come and find us?" he persisted.

"Yes, Keith. If anyone took you or Stephanie or Beth away, we would find you and bring you back home." She tucked him snuggly into bed, kissed him gently on his forehead, and tiptoed downstairs.

Jonathan, Mark, and the adults were gathered, as usual, for the evening television newscast. David looked up at his wife who sat down beside him. "All quiet now?"

"Yes. They're all asleep, finally. Oh, David, they are so afraid they'll be taken back to juvenile hall. Beth just can't fall asleep unless I sit there and hold her. She's terrified I won't be there when she wakes up."

Rachel looked down at Daniel napping beside her on the couch. "I love him so, Pam, but sometimes I'm sorry we have him. Who knows what horrors my son will have to live through?"

"He's so little, he doesn't understand, Rachel," said the pastor. "He only knows you love him."

"But later, Frank—"

"If there is a later." Joe sighed, pondering the television announcer's words. "War, pillage, robbery, massacre, hunger? Why should I, or my son, be spared?"

"Seven years," David reminded them. "And part of that, two years at least, is already past."

"Yes, Joe. This old world isn't going to last long enough for Daniel to suffer."

"Frank, I'm surprised at you. You've always warned us not to force interpretations. Now you sound as certain as Tom Braden, or—" Sandy hesitated. "Or Bob, when he talked about the Rapture."

Pam noticed that Frank touched Sandy's hand absently as he answered. "Yes, you're right. We don't know. And yet, I do believe God gave us the prophecies to help us. He wanted us to be prepared."

"Then why are they so deliberately obscure?"

Frank shrugged. "Maybe he wanted people to

have to live only by faith. He wants us to live by faith, even now. If we did know all his plans, if we did know the future, there would be no faith."

"And no free will, either," David commented.

"No, I guess not. If we could see the future clearly, we'd be gods, not men. And I've always thought that was the original sin. Eve wanted knowledge so she would be like God."

The voice from the television set droned on. It was the same news every night. The reports minimized the outbreaks of lawlessness that marred the secretary general's uneasy peace. The news dwelt on the rebuilding effort, reforestation, the promise of good harvests. But disturbing bits of information persisted in slipping through.

As the adults pondered Frank's concept of original sin, Mark, sprawled on the floor, looked up. "Mom, is the war going to come here?"

"The war is a long way away, Mark, in India."

"It's the other side of the world, silly," Jonathan scoffed. "They don't have any rockets. They don't even have ships or airplanes. They were all wrecked in the earthquakes. Don't you know anything?"

"Jon, don't make fun of your brother. He has a right to be afraid." Sandy rumpled both boys' hair. "Mark, the Chinese are starving. They are marching across Asia looking for food. We should pray for them."

"Pastor Frank, doesn't the Bible say a war comes after the locusts?"

"Yes, Mark, it does. But it doesn't necessarily say the war will extend over the whole world. A lot of people are being killed now, but I think there will be another period of peace soon."

"Why, Frank?"

"Well, Rachel, the Beast hasn't actually been revealed."

Sandy interrupted. "What about the secretary, Frank? He survived the death stroke."

"Yes, and I'm virtually certain he is the Antichrist. What I meant was that he hasn't actually taken up all his authority yet. When he does, I think we'll have a short period of peace."

"He got a peace treaty for Israel right after the first earthquake." Joe offered. "The building of the new temple has begun on top of the ruins of the Dome of the Rock. The two witnesses are already preaching."

"That's true, Joe, yet—"

"I thought we'd agreed we weren't supposed to set dates," Pam remarked. Just then the familiar face of the secretary appeared on the television screen, capturing the curiosity of the Cristman household.

"We suffer with the hordes that are coming out of the East," began Crosetti. "We understand their need. We know they fight for food. Nonetheless, they must be stopped. They have already overrun Asia and are moving toward Western Europe by way of Iran and Iraq. Appeals to their leadership, such as it is, have failed. Therefore, I have decided that they must be stopped by any means necessary."

"What! What is he getting at?"

"Shhh, David." Pam really didn't want to hear Crosetti's words, but she knew she must.

The secretary continued: "A United Nations

peace-keeping force is now being organized for dispatch to the plains of Iraq. This force will be fully armed with every defense at our disposal. The Chinese army will be given ample opportunity to disperse; but if it persists in its march, it will be destroyed."

Pam gasped in disbelief, glancing at the astonished faces around her. "Nuclear weapons? Does he mean he will use nuclear weapons against an army on foot and armed with only clubs and a few rifles?"

"It sounds like it," David said sadly.

The news over the next few weeks seemed even more propagandized than usual. A great deal of time was given to the horrors inflicted by the Asian masses. Everywhere they moved they stole every scrap of edible vegetation. Livestock were slaughtered and eaten, or driven off to trample neighboring fields. And each village they came to was leveled by their march.

Diseases followed them—diseases long dormant in the West—typhus, cholera, bubonic plague. And terror preceded them, fanned by televised scenes of the old, the sick, the children . . . dying mercilessly beneath clubs or horses' hooves.

Secretary Crosetti had promised this would be stopped. And, suddenly, word came that it had. The United Nations' forces had met the Asian movement head-on, in the heart of the once-fertile crescent between the Tigris and the Euphrates. And the few who survived the attack were scattered.

How the Asians had been stopped was never made known officially, but the world was satisfied that they had been stopped. Civilization, in spite of all that had happened in the past few years, seemed safe again.

However, there were rumors out of the Middle East reporting that refugees—Chinese, Thai, Indian— were straggling into Jerusalem. These people were truly pitiable, it was said. They had been skin and bones before, but now the skin shredded off the bones. They had gaping, raw sores. They couldn't keep food down if they were lucky enough to be fed. Many had gone blind. Many died of severe anemia or acute leukemia.

The refugees told stories of a bright, white light in the sky and fireballs a mile wide. Undoubtedly, these were victims of nuclear attack. Yet even those who had seen them expressed gratitude to the secretary for preserving the world from anarchy.

And, again, Crosetti had saved Israel. There was even talk in Jerusalem that he had a Jewish mother and that Crosetti himself might be the Messiah.

The secretary modestly declined to take credit, thanking the people again for their support and their prayers. But all over the world his picture appeared in stores, offices, and public buildings. People wore his picture on pins or chains around their necks. Even the news reporters no longer spoke of the actions of the United Nations or of the Security Council. It was always the secretary who decided, who moved, who accomplished.

Tom Braden, too, gave Crosetti credit for the improving conditions. "You have to admit, Frank," he insisted, when Frank encountered him one day in Little Valley, "the man knows how to get things done.

Who else could have organized reconstruction like the secretary has?"

Frank nodded absently as Tom rattled on.

"You remember how bad things were right after the comet hit—the locusts and all. Then Crosetti recovered from his injuries and took over, and things got better right away. It's a miracle. Yes, Frank, a miracle."

"Has it occurred to you, Tom, that it's been a little *too* miraculous?"

"I thought you believed in miracles, Frank. You used to preach about them quite a lot. I even hear tell you've experienced one or two yourself."

"Yes, I have, Tom. But you know there are miracles from God and miracles from Satan. Crosetti is a powerful leader, but the Bible describes the Antichrist as a great deceiver. It strongly indicates a brief period of peace at the beginning of his deceitful reign."

Tom sneered. "Frank, you don't still believe those fairy tales, do you?"

"Tom, we've had earthquakes. We've had fire from heaven. The great rock thrown into the sea. The locusts. You know the Bible, Tom. You know these things were all foretold."

"So was the Rapture. That didn't happen. Where is the Christ, Frank?"

"He will come, Tom. Some of us were wrong about the Rapture, obviously, but Jesus will come."

"Maybe he has."

"You mean the Rapture happened, but we were left behind?"

"No, Frank. I mean we have a man here on earth

who, almost literally, came back from the dead. You yourself admitted that he's done miracles in putting the world back together again. Maybe he's our returned Lord."

"Tom, don't say that!" Frank recoiled. "Don't even think it."

Tom shrugged. "I didn't say I believed it. Personally, I think he's just a very smart, very powerful man who's doing a fantastic job. But if God really did cause all those disasters, maybe we're better off with Crosetti."

The Cristman household knew better. They were appalled at the adulation Crosetti was receiving. Yet even they were enjoying the respite his rule provided.

"I know building a house sounds a little foolish," Joe explained one July morning, "But even if it's only for a year we'd like to do it."

"Yes, David," Rachel agreed. "The children are getting older, and this house is hardly designed for a family of twelve."

David nodded. "We don't really have much privacy, any of us. Why not finish the other house?" He glanced at Sandy.

"I think it's a great idea. Joe and Rachel need a place of their own."

"You're sure you wouldn't mind, Sandy? It's really your house, and we haven't any money—"

"The framing is up and the roof half on." Sandy smiled. "It's about the time the house was finished and lived in."

And so one warm September evening, Joe and Rachel invited their friends to a housewarming. Frank dedicated the cottage, and the lives within it, to the Lord's service; and each voiced thanksgiving that the time of terror had ended, if only temporarily.

Late that evening Frank found Sandy alone on the porch of the new house. "This has been a rough night for you, hasn't it, Sandy? I know this house was to have been yours and Bob's."

"Yes, and I have been thinking about Bob. But I'm fine now." She turned and looked up at Frank. "I feel like this is the end of that part of my life. The house doesn't belong to us anymore. There isn't any 'us' anymore."

"What about the boys?"

"They're both growing up so fast. Jon's a young man already. Even Mark is not my 'little boy' anymore. I loved Bob, Frank, but he's gone, and the boys are already pulling away."

"And you?"

"I guess I'm just me. I'm not Mrs. Peters any longer, or even Jon and Mark's mother. I'm me, Sandy Peters."

"I like Sandy Peters very much." Frank whispered the words as he cupped her face in his calloused hands. "You know that, don't you?"

"Yes, Frank. I think I know that. And I know I couldn't have reached this point, this peace, without you. Thank you for being there. Thank you." She paused. "Thank you for caring, and for waiting."

Frank gathered her into his arms; they knew, both of them, that they were no longer alone.

A few days later, Sandy stood outside the ranch house plucking chickens. She could still feel the warmth of Frank's arms about her. *I'd forgotten*, she mused. *I'd forgotten how much I missed Bob, physically. I've learned to cope, relearned, I guess, with making all the decisions. And I've gone to bed too tired to lie awake missing him.*

She looked out across the meadow, noticing how the aspen waved in the autumn wind, even as the spreading black oaks scarcely trembled. *Frank. Bob. How could I love two men so much who are so different? Why? I know I loved Bob. Do I really love Frank that way, or am I just afraid of being alone?*

Sandy hadn't married young. Her and Pam's mother had died when Pam was a kindergartner. Sandy, twelve years older, had spent twelve years being a mother to her little sister. Then Bob came into her life, and he took the burden. *I guess a lot of women would have called him a male chauvinist. He decided what we had for dinner, and what I wore to church. They didn't understand, I guess, that I wanted that, needed it. I was tired of being in charge.*

She bent to gather wind-scattered, wet, chicken feathers. *And he left me, just when I needed him most. So . . .* She shrugged and picked up the half-plucked chicken. *So I went back to being Sandy in charge, didn't I?*

Do I want Frank to take over? Is that why I want him? She looked out toward the woods again. *He won't. That isn't his way. Bob was as strong as the oak, and as unbending. Frank's weak. No.* She remembered the morning he had faced down the satanists. *No, he's not weak. Meek. Meek, maybe, and gentle. He'll never force his will. But in his own way he is even stronger than Bob. He can weather the storm.*

The breeze caressed her, blowing a stray hair across her cheek as a gentle hand might. Frank's gentle hand. She smiled.

"Want to let me in on the secret, Sandy?" Pam asked, as the kitchen door snapped shut behind her.

"What secret?"

"Whatever it is that's making you so cheerful. You don't usually sing when you're pulling pinfeathers."

Sandy flipped the plucked hen into the dishpan and took another one out of the bucket of scalding water. "I didn't realize it showed."

"Ever since Joe and Rachel's housewarming, you've been skipping around here like a colt turned loose in the spring." Pam picked up the carving knife and began cutting and cleaning the chicken. "And I love it. Want to share your good news?"

Sandy hesitated. "I'm not sure, Pam. Maybe it's too soon, but . . . well . . . Frank and I had a long talk after the party."

"I knew it!" Pam hugged her sister despite the soggy chicken leg in her hand. "I knew you would wake up one of these days."

"Wake up? You mean you had it all figured out already?"

"Sandy, I've got eyes, though I've been wondering if *you* did. Why, Frank's been in love with you for months. Since before he moved out here, I think."

"Yes, I guess I have known he cared. But there was Bob."

"It's been a long time, Sandy."

"Only a little over two years. I feel a little guilty, even now, about loving someone else."

"A lot over two years, and it's been more like a lifetime. Sandy, you mustn't feel guilty. It's wonderful."

Sandy's slight frown fled. "I think one of the things I love most about Frank is his patience. He waited, Pam, for me to let him know that I felt free, at last, from Bob's memory."

"I've wondered, sometimes, how I'd bear it if anything happened to David. I can't imagine life without him. I can't imagine loving anyone else. And yet, noticing the way Frank looks at you, the tenderness in his eyes, I've praised God for sending him to you. You've needed someone so much."

"But Frank isn't just someone, Pam. I was afraid

of that, but I'm sure I love him for himself, that we are right for each other."

Pam nodded, as her sister continued, "He's so different from Bob. Sometimes I wonder how I could love two men who are so very different. I need Frank very much, Pam, and I love him very much. But it's different this time."

"Frank needs you too. Is that what you mean, maybe?"

"Yes, I think so. Oh, Bob and I needed each other in a way, and we did have a good marriage, Pam. But I was so dependent on him, I can't ever remember his needing me. Oh, as a wife, yes, and a mother to the boys, but not as a person. It was enough, then. But Frank isn't like that. Frank needs me as much as I need him."

"Sandy, it's a different world. We're all different. You're different."

"Yes, I guess I am." Sandy dropped her gaze to avoid her sister's eyes. "I love him very much, Pam. And I want to help him and encourage him. And he has what I need now. He loves me. He loves the boys too. In fact, in some ways he's already a father to them."

"Yes, I've noticed they seem to go to him with their problems more than to David. I think David feels a little hurt, in fact."

"Oh, no. David's been good, more than good, to us all. He mustn't feel the boys don't love him."

"Oh, he doesn't. It's just that he's always been Uncle Dave. Maybe they've gone to Frank more as a pastor. But the important thing is, they are close to him. They won't resent him as a stepfather when you and Frank get married."

Sandy dropped the second chicken into the waiting dishpan. "*If* we get married."

"But I thought ... I mean ... you love each other. You need each other. The boys will be delighted. Why not?"

"Among other things, he hasn't asked me."

"I'm sure that's only a matter of time, like a few days," Pam said dryly.

"No, it's not just that. It's the times. I mean, we wouldn't want children, at our ages, and with the end so close."

"The end *probably* so close," Pam protested. "But, as Joe said the other night, it could be another two thousand years."

"You don't believe that any more than I do, and neither does Frank."

"But there are reasons for marriage other than having children, Sandy."

"We already have companionship. Financially, well, if the truth were told, we're both living off you and David."

"Don't ever think that. You both put every bit as much work into this place as we do. You earn everything you get."

"I won't quibble about wages or investment, but it isn't that simple. I know Frank feels a little uncomfortable about living here. But what choice is there?"

"There's plenty of room for another house, Sandy, and plenty of wood and land. And Frank is our pastor too. We still believe those who serve the Lord deserve their living from that."

"I'm afraid Frank will have to come to terms with that problem himself, Pam, if he needs to, or wants to."

"If it is keeping you two from fulfilling your relationship, Sandy, then we have to help him resolve it. I'll talk to David."

"No, Pam, please. Frank wouldn't want that."

"I suppose you're right. Anyhow, I know it will work out for you."

"It has. We're happy just knowing we love each other. We don't need marriage for that."

"You don't?" Pam took Sandy's hand in her own. "You don't really mean that, do you?"

Sandy bit her lip shyly as she fumbled for words. It was still hard for her to discuss such things, even with her sister. "We can manage, Pam. We don't have to—"

"Oh, Sandy, you silly kid. There's nothing wrong with sex. There's nothing wrong with wanting someone physically. You and Frank have every right to want a marriage relationship."

Sandy smiled, grateful that Pam had focused on her unspoken desire. "Yes, Pam. I do want to marry him."

The two women would have been surprised to know that Frank and David were having a similar discussion at the same time. They were digging potatoes when Frank broached the subject. "Dave, I can't tell you how much it's meant, your taking me in like this, keeping me, making me feel needed when the church fell apart."

"What do you mean, making you feel needed? You *are* needed, Frank. Without you and Joe we'd never be able to keep the ranch producing. We'd all starve."

"Would you, with fewer mouths to feed? David, I feel I should move on, find work, now that the economy is getting back to normal."

"Where? Doing what?"

"There must be people somewhere who still want to hear the gospel and can pay a preacher a living wage."

"I haven't heard of any."

"Well, I can farm. You've taught me something about that. I can cut wood."

"You're doing that here. Frank, I think I know what you're getting at."

"I doubt it," Frank snapped suddenly. "I'm sorry, David. I didn't mean to be so sharp, but I don't think you do understand. It's something personal. I need to be independent. I need to be able to take care of myself again before I can—" He stabbed his pitchfork desperately into the ground. "Before I can take care of anyone else."

"Sandy? Come on, Frank. It's obvious the way you two feel about each other. And I do understand how you feel. You can't ask her to marry you unless you feel you can support her and the boys."

Frank stooped, picking up potatoes and hiding his face at the same time. "Okay, David. You've stated the problem. So, I don't see any choice but to move on and try to find a job."

"I do. We'll draw up a contract and formalize our situation here. Frank, I need you. It will be a partnership. You've already contributed your car, some of the chickens, seeds, tools, and a whale of a lot of sweat equity."

"Wait a minute. It's your land, your house, your livestock. There's no comparison."

"I'll pay you wages; you pay me rent. Cut your own wood and build your own house, and pay me for the wood and the land out of your wages. Whatever you want. But don't move out and leave us."

"I know you're just being your usual generous self."

"I'm not, Frank. I'm being very practical. We need every pair of hands we have to survive. We need your spiritual guidance too. And, Frank, things are going to get worse again. We're going to need each other. What if something happened to me? What would Pam and the little kids do? And what would Sandy do? Think about it, Frank."

Frank kicked the soft soil again, stooped, and added more potatoes to his sack. "I'll think about it, David."

But there was little time for thought. A few days later the nightly news brought the announcement they had almost stopped expecting. The benign face of Secretary Crosetti filled the television screen once again. Though conditions had improved greatly, he explained, much of the world still lay in ruins.

"In order to facilitate rationing, as well as to

restore economic order and enforce basic law," the secretary announced, "the existing registry system must be tightened. All registration cards will be turned in and replaced by a new system of identification."

"Can it be?" Pam gasped.

Frank responded to the fear on Sandy's face. "If this is it, our respite is over," he said.

Their fears were confirmed as a reporter proceeded to detail the secretary's new order. "All existing identity cards will be replaced by an indelible tattoo on the palm of the right hand. In those instances where a person has lost his right hand, or if desired for any other reason, the tattoo may be placed on the forehead instead."

They stared at the TV screen, amazed at the brazen defiance of the man who had issued the decree.

"He admitted it," Pam breathed. "He's told us, openly, that he's the Antichrist."

"Hush," David whispered sharply. "Listen."

"As of January 1 of next year," the impersonal voice continued, "No official business can be conducted by any individual not so identified." And official business, since the Middle East war of the past spring, had included all commercial as well as legal transactions.

"What is the tattoo?" Pam wondered when the shock had begun to wear off. She assumed it would be an individual number, probably the one on the card being turned in.

"We'll find out soon enough," Frank shuddered.

"We've got three months, as I see it, to become so self-sufficient that we can survive without any outside help. It's going to be us and God now."

Late that night, after the Cristmans and Stenbergs had finally gone to bed, exhausted, Frank and Sandy still sat side by side on the porch swing. A chill much more intense than the fall evening's breeze drew them close. Sandy's head fit Frank's shoulder as if it had always rested there. His arm held her close as her relaxed body pressed against his own.

How can I be so happy? she asked herself. *What right do I have to so much peace when the world is in such agony?* She stirred ever so slightly.

"Sandy," Frank murmured. "Sandy, are you all right?"

"Perfect."

"Perfect? Yes, you're perfect, and I love you. But you're worried."

"I guess I'm worried because I'm not worried." She raised her head and looked at him. "Frank, I feel so good here with you. And I feel guilty, because the world is coming to an end and I'm acting like a schoolgirl in love."

"You too." He brushed a stray curl from her forehead, and their eyes met. "But, Sandy, we do have a decision we must make. I haven't put it into words yet. I wanted to get ready, to make a home for you and the boys before I asked you."

She held her breath. *Now, with so little time left?* she wondered.

"Sandy, there are terrible times ahead, and there

are only three months for us to prepare. Will you marry me, Sandy, now?"

"Now?"

"After the mark it will be too late. We cannot accept the mark of the Beast, so legal marriage will be impossible for us then. If something should happen . . . Sandy, I have very little to leave, but I would want it to be yours. And if . . . oh my God, Sandy . . . if it should be you, what would happen to the boys?"

Sandy gasped then at the thought she had tried to avoid.

"Sandy, it's horrible to imagine, but you would want me to have the right to care for them, wouldn't you?"

20

"Jonathan, is something wrong?" Mark had hugged his mother, grinning with delight at her news, but Jonathan still sat quietly beside her on the porch swing.

"Jon, we want you to be part of our decision. Don't you want me to marry your mother?"

"I'm sorry, Pastor Frank. I guess I was remembering Dad, that day." Jonathan blinked as a tear struggled to escape. "I've missed him so much, and I know Mom has too."

Sandy started to interrupt, but the boy, fast becoming a young man, continued: "Pastor Frank, I think it's wonderful. Mom's so much happier already. And I—" Jonathan stood then, bit his lip, and faced Frank. The words came hard, but they came from his heart. "Frank, I love you too."

Frank took the boy's extended hand, then pulled

THE REVELATION

Jonathan to him with an embrace. And the young man, still much a boy, yielded to the loving gesture.

"Sandy, sit down here a few minutes," Pam insisted, as Sandy drew the dishwater after breakfast the next morning. "We have to make plans if you're to be married in two weeks."

Pam tapped a pencil against a sheet of paper. "You're going to be married here, of course. We'll still have mums in bloom. David can round up the guests with the wagon and bring them out from town to save gas."

Sandy laughed as she hadn't in years. "Whoa, Pam. This isn't going to be your standard wedding celebration, you know."

"But the church—"

"I know the church isn't usable; I would have liked to be married there in the grove. But you know religious ceremonies aren't recognized anymore, and the whole idea of being married right away is so that it will be legal. We'll have to do that at the courthouse."

"But you'll have a Christian wedding, Sandy. You have to."

"We have to, but, Pam, you're leaving something out of your plans. Who's going to marry us?"

"Good grief, Sandy. I hadn't even thought of that. Little Valley only had three churches before. The Reverend Smythe—" She wrinkled her nose slightly. "Well, the Reverend has left town. And Father Keeney wouldn't, I don't think, even if you wanted him to."

"No. Actually Frank likes him. He really seems to

know the Lord himself, but he's stubborn about Catholic dogma. And we couldn't, either of us, compromise on that."

"Then who, Sandy? Surely there's another Christian minister somewhere nearby."

"Frank and I have talked about it quite a bit. Pam, I know you'll be disappointed, but Frank has an old friend in the county seat, a pastor he went to seminary with. We thought we'd have the civil ceremony first, at the courthouse, and then go to his home for his blessing."

"But we can't all leave the ranch at once. Hmmm." Pam pursed her lips. "Sandy, why can't he come here?"

"Like all of us, he'll be hoarding gas against the first of the year. Since we have to go down there anyhow, we really can't ask him to make the trip too."

Two weeks later the hay wagon made the thirty-mile trip to the county seat. The wagon was laden with fresh-cut chrysanthemums in gold, bright copper and clear yellow, which also concealed the jars of milk and crocks of butter they took for Frank's friend.

Pam was her sister's matron of honor. David drove, and was Frank's best man, while Jonathan gave his mother away. Mark and the minister's wife were the only other guests. It seemed best for Joe and Rachel to stay home with the four small children.

Before leaving the courthouse the newlyweds filed Frank's application to legally adopt Mark and Jonathan. They could only pray that the process could be completed before or without the permanent identification they had vowed to avoid at any cost.

THE REVELATION

Though they returned to the ranch immediately, Sandy and Frank did manage a few days' honeymoon. They camped in a tiny, brookside glade at one corner of the ranch. God blessed them with Indian summer days; they fished, talked, and walked hand in hand under the golden aspen and deep green redwoods.

At night they nestled in a downy sleeping bag, counted the stars, and forgot for a little while the coming trouble. "I know that God is an awesome judge, Sandy," Frank whispered, holding his bride close. "But all I can think of right now is how wonderful his mercy is. How much he cares for us. How much he must love us, you and me, to have given us to each other."

But their honeymoon nest was discovered, after only three days, by Keith and Stephanie. The youngsters protested they were only looking for Snoopy, the cat, and her new kittens.

"Shall we just give up and go home with them?" Sandy sighed.

Frank had already begun pulling tent stakes. "We could just send them home, I guess, but I feel a little guilty anyhow, taking time off when we have so much to do in the next two months."

That night David and Frank drew up the formal partnership agreement giving Frank part ownership of the ranch. "Now it's official, and you can't say I'm supporting you anymore," David said, handing his new partner a copy of the single-page document. "And it's a fair deal, more than fair."

"I'm not sure of that, Dave. I still say your terms

were too generous. I'm not putting up all that much cash; and anyhow, what's cash worth these days?"

"Cash is worth a lot more now than it will be after New Year's, to us anyhow. By spending it wisely for seed and tools and as much food and gas as we can get our hands on, maybe we can survive until the Lord does come."

Christmas at the ranch this year was more lavish than it had been since the first great quake. "We might as well spend what we have," David and Frank told their wives. "We certainly won't be doing any shopping after the holidays."

Stephanie and Beth both hugged store-bought dolls, not caring in the least that the curly-haired treasures were secondhand. Keith was too overjoyed at actually owning his own bicycle to realize that that bike was soon to be his chief means of transportation.

Mark and Jonathan did understand the meaning of their gifts. "Thank you, Frank," Mark had cried with the eagerness of youth as he unwrapped the rifle.

Jonathan's appreciation was more thoughtful. "Frank," he said soberly, inspecting the weapon, "I guess we'll be doing some hunting from now on." But later, privately, he questioned his stepfather. "I thought guns couldn't be bought legally."

"They can't, Son."

Jonathan looked puzzled, but he nodded slowly. "We don't always obey the laws anymore, do we?"

"Not anymore. Jon, things are going to be very bad after the new law goes into effect. We won't be able to buy or sell anything, at least not legally. Legally, we will all be 'nonpersons.' You do understand why, don't you?"

"Yes, I think so. Most everybody says it's nothing, just a new way to make sure everybody really is who he says he is. But we believe it's the mark of the Beast, and so we can't accept it. Frank, are you sure the mark is really wrong?"

"I do know the Bible says no one who takes the mark of the Beast or worships the Beast can enter God's Kingdom. Somehow, just accepting that tattoo implies worship."

"And you're sure Secretary Crosetti is the Beast?"

"Secretary Crosetti was given dictatorial power by the United Nations. He assured Israel that it would be secure as a nation and supported rebuilding of the temple. Then he died, by all normal definitions, and came back to life. And now he's demanding that every man and woman in the world be tattooed with a personal identification number consisting of three sets of six digits each."

Jonathan nodded. "Literal fulfillment, right down the line. I know. Yet everybody in town talks about how wonderful Secretary Crosetti is and how he's bringing peace and prosperity out of all the troubles."

"Jon, what do you believe?" The old doubts edged into Frank's mind as he waited for Jonathan's answer.

"I believe the Bible." The weight lifted from Frank's heart as the boy continued: "I believe in God and in his Word."

"Then you know what we must do, Jon. You understand that if we were to let anyone tattoo that number on us in obedience to the secretary, it would be an act of deliberate disobedience to God."

"Yes, Frank. And if we refuse the mark, God will take care of us."

"If I were not absolutely sure of that, I think I would die of sheer terror."

"Frank, something else has been bothering me. Since you and Mom got married I've been thinking more about Dad. Not comparing, just remembering."

"That's all right, Jon. I don't want you ever to forget your father."

"He was always so sure of everything."

"He was sure of his faith and of his God. And so we can be sure he is with God now."

"Yes, I know that. But, Frank, he was so sure about the Rapture. He couldn't believe the Tribulation had started. Now you believe we're living in it; I've studied Revelation, and I believe so too. Still, if Dad was wrong about the Rapture, what about the rest?"

"Many people with lots more years and more knowledge than you have been asking that question, Jon. We must all be very careful about what we believe. We must never trust men's interpretations, Jon—our own or anyone else's. But there is a bottom line, Jon. There is a foundation of clear, plain truth in God's Word."

"But different people read it differently. Even Secretary Crosetti claims to read the Bible, so how can we be sure what it means?"

"Oh, Jon, if only I could set down absolute truth in a few sentences, a few words for you, your brother, and all the people of the world. Most of the Bible is clear, Jon. What is clear we can depend on, absolutely. There is a God, one God, who created all the universe and created man in his image. Man rebelled against God, so we are all sinners by nature. Jesus Christ is God, incarnate in human flesh, and he died for our sins. As for the rest, I just don't have all the answers. But, Jon, he promised to give us wisdom. We will know what we need to know, when we need to know it."

Frank's anguish compelled him to hold Jonathan close as he prayed silently for that wisdom. "One thing I do know, Son, beyond any doubt. Job said it first, and it's still the truth. 'Though He slay me, yet will I trust Him.'"

"I'm sorry, David." Ed Downing, the grocer, offered his marked hand, but David did not take it. "I'm sorry, but I just can't do business with you anymore."

"You've always carried our cheese, Ed. You know it's good."

"I know, but if the inspectors found cheese in my store without their stamp on it, they could close me down on the spot. You understand, David. I respect your principles, but I have a family to support."

"So do I," David answered bitterly. "All I need is some aspirin. The children have the flu or something. They're feverish. The cheese is worth so much more."

"Not your cheese, David. I'm sorry about the kids, but I can't take the chance of putting unapproved merchandise on my shelves."

David turned away. "David," Ed called after him.

THE REVELATION

"David, is it really all that important, a little number tattooed on your hand? What harm could it do?"

David's shoulders sagged as he left the store. Main Street looked almost normal, he thought. Cars inched along between the town's two stoplights, honking at stray dogs and pedestrians. People stepped into stores and came out with parcels. They smiled at one another and talked about the return of good times.

"David, David Cristman," someone called.

David looked up to see Jeff Conners, a former Little Valley church deacon. "Oh, hello, Jeff."

"David, how've you been? I haven't seen you in town since before Christmas."

"We keep pretty busy at the ranch with spring planting and all." His eyes avoided Jeff's extended hand. "You folks doing all right?"

"Sure, great. Isn't it miraculous the way things are coming back? We'll be seeing more of you now, I suppose."

"Why?" David asked.

"Well, with the increased gas ration you'll be able to use your car again. I know it takes a long time to come in by wagon."

He had no idea, David realized. His answer was mechanical. "We get no gas, Jeff."

"No gas? Come on, David, don't tell me you're one of those rebels?"

"If it is rebellion to obey God," he admitted, "then I guess I'm a rebel."

"I thought you had better sense." Jeff glanced at David's hands. "Now, this Crosetti—here's a man who has almost single-handedly held civilization together in the face of unprecedented natural disasters and invasion by millions of barbarians, and yet a handful of stubborn fools like you accuse him of being some sort of devil."

"Jeff, you've studied the Bible as much as I have. You've even taught Sunday school. Surely you realize that Crosetti is almost certainly the Antichrist. And if he is, that tattoo you wear with so little concern makes you a condemned man. I can understand people who never knew, but how could you do this?"

"For Pete's sake, David, where is your common sense? How could any man do what Crosetti's done unless God was with him?"

Jeff strode off, and David rode slowly home to Pam and the sick children.

"Don't fret, David," Pam soothed, when he told her he'd failed to get the aspirin. "They'll be better tomorrow. The Lord is looking after them."

Keith was still burning with fever the next morning, and now Rachel appeared with Daniel. "I hoped you had a little aspirin, Sandy," she said.

Sandy shook her head. "Dave took cheese into town yesterday to trade for some, but Ed turned him down."

"The mark?"

"Yes," Frank told her. "Seems farm produce has to be inspected. No inspection stamp, no sale. And, of course, you can't get your stuff inspected if you can't identify yourself 'properly.'"

"Pam's upstairs giving Keith a sponge bath," Sandy said. "Why don't you take Daniel up there and put him to bed? You can share nursing chores."

After a few minutes Frank closed his Bible and reached for his sweater. "Sandy," he said, "I've been meaning to go into town and call on some of our friends. I think I'll go today. Maybe I can get some aspirin somewhere."

A cold March wind blew as he knocked on the Braden door. Peggy answered, but stood silent in the open doorway.

"Aren't you going to ask me in, Peggy?"

"Pastor," she stumbled. "Pastor Frank. I, ah, I guess so. Come in if you like."

She stepped aside, and he followed her into the familiar living room. "What's wrong, Peggy? Somehow I don't think you're glad to see me."

He realized Tom sat, unmoving, in a deep chair. "Hello, Tom. How are you doing?" Frank forced a cheerful tone into the stony silence.

"Hullo. Suppose you came to check up on us."

"Oh, Tom, you know Frank better than that. I'm sorry, Pastor. It's just that things haven't been going too well lately. I lost my job, you know."

Frank was shocked. "Lost your job? But Peggy, there's a nursing shortage, and you're one of the best."

"Not anymore. I don't exist. Peggy Braden is an R.N. with twenty years experience, but I'm not Peggy Braden. I'm nobody." Her voice was harsh. It was as if she were blaming Frank. And in a sense she was. "I didn't take the mark. I didn't get their tattoo, so I'm no longer employed."

"But, Peggy, you didn't take the mark because you know the Lord forbids it. He won't let us starve,

Peggy. We belong to him, and we're obeying him. Just trust him to provide."

"He's providing, all right." Tom stood, then, and thrust his right hand out in bitter greeting. "That's how he's providing. One good thing's come out of all this anyhow. I'm supporting my wife again."

An ugly ulcer seared the palm of Tom's hand, but the hated number burned within the sore. "Now I'm working. We're being taken care of all right, but does she care? Does she appreciate it? No."

Frank drew back as Peggy pleaded with her husband. "Tom, please. Please stop, Tom."

She sobbed as she turned to Frank. "He was desperate. He isn't worshiping that devil. He did it for me, so I'd have enough to eat. Can't you understand that? Can't God understand that?"

Frank wanted to flee, run from the horrible ulcer and its more horrible significance. "I can understand it, Peggy," he answered sadly. "I can, and maybe God can too. But God demands obedience. And he told us no one who took that mark would be saved."

"Saved from what, Frank? Saved from public ridicule? Saved from going underground, like you? Saved from starvation?"

Frank merely shook his head. Tom was beyond his reach now. Tom continued his harangue. "No, God didn't save me from his judgment, so now I'm relying on myself and on someone who seems to have some power, the secretary."

Frank retreated, and Peggy followed him out the door. "Thank you for coming, Frank. I know you're shocked. I suppose I should leave him, but he's my husband. I know what he's done. And he wants me to do it too, Pastor. What can I do? I love him. I can't help that. What should I do?"

Frank took her hands in his as he prayed silently: *Why does everyone expect answers from me, when I have none to give?* "Peggy, I don't know. But no matter what happens, I know God is in control. No matter how impossible our circumstances seem, he is still there, and he is still watching over us."

"Is Tom lost, Pastor? He knew the Lord. He was saved. Pastor Frank, I'm sure he was a Christian. Now he's done this, this thing." Her eyes filled and her voice quivered. "Pastor Frank, is my husband going to hell because he didn't want to see me starve?"

Frank couldn't bear to look into those eyes. He looked down at her trembling hands and his own and just shook his head.

Reluctantly, Frank turned from her and climbed into the surrey. But as he picked up the reins, he remembered his original errand. Peggy still stood on the porch. He stepped down and walked back to her.

"Peggy, this sounds terrible, I know, but I came here today partly to ask for your help."

"Anything I can do, Pastor. There are so few of us." She glanced in the window, but Tom still sat stiffly in his chair. "We have to help each other all we can."

"Peggy, the Cristman kids and Daniel Stenberg have bad cases of the flu. Keith and Daniel are burning up with fever."

She shook her head. "No, Frank. I can't go out there with you. He'd kill me, I think. And I haven't any medicine."

"A little aspirin, Peggy? Just a little aspirin to bring their temperatures down."

Suddenly she smiled. "Aspirin, of course. Yes, Frank, I have a full bottle." She glanced inside again. "But Tom wouldn't like it. Frank, go around to the side of the house. I'll hand it out the bathroom window."

In mid-May, David and Pam received notice that the final adoption hearing for the Turner children had been scheduled. "I'd almost managed to forget," Pam whispered. "David, what will happen?"

"It will be all right, Pam. God will take care of it."

"Do you think we should just ignore the hearing?" David asked Frank that evening.

"If you don't show up, they will almost certainly come looking for you."

"Yes, David. They'd come and take them, like they did last time. I know they would. David, we have to go to the hearing."

"The children are fine, Pam, and they obviously love you," said Sandy. "The judge will let you keep them."

"Without the mark?"

"Children aren't required to have the mark," Sandy reminded her.

"But we are," Pam sighed. "The judge will ask to see our tattoos, and when we don't have them, he will take our babies away from us."

"I can't believe the Lord intends that you lose those children, Pam," Frank assured her. "He loves them, and he must want them in your care."

Pam clung to David and said, "Frank's right, darling. God sent them to us to take care of, and he won't let them be taken away."

David stroked her hair lightly. "It will take a miracle, Pam."

"Then we'll start praying for a miracle," Frank said, slipping to his knees as he, Sandy, Pam, and David joined hands and pleaded with their God.

The next morning David and Pam, with an excited trio of children, drove to the courthouse.

"Mommy Pam and Daddy Dave are going to be our really, truly Mommy and Daddy," Stephanie explained to her younger brother and sister. "They're going to 'dopt us."

"Then the social worker welfare lady can't ever get us again," Keith added with all the certainty of childhood.

Pam clutched David's clammy hand as they started up the courthouse steps. "Remember," he whispered, "God can do a miracle."

As they started to enter the courthouse door, an armed guard blocked their path. "Name, number, and business, please."

"I'm David Cristman. We're here to finalize adoption of our three children." David pulled the notice from his pocket.

The guard read the notice quickly. "Your I.D., please?"

David took out the pass that had been issued the year before, but he knew as he did so that it wouldn't be enough. The guard stared, then grunted. "This isn't any good anymore. I have to see your official I.D. Your hand, please."

"We don't want to cause any trouble," Pam interrupted, "but we have an appointment with Judge Roberts."

"Not if you haven't an I.D. number. No one gets in without a number."

"Is there someone we could talk to, someone in authority who might be able to resolve this?" David asked patiently, though he already knew the answer.

"Where have you people been the last six months? You know you can't do any business here without an I.D." The guard was turning nasty now. "No mark, no business with the court."

Evidently his sharp tone was counter to public policy, because a uniformed official appeared at the doorway and began questioning him. After a brief discussion, the officer turned to Pam and David. "I really do not understand how you can have appeared here this way. Surely you knew you could not possibly be admitted without your I.D. However, it is not our intention to hinder the business of the court. I'll see what I can do."

It was over half an hour before the officer reappeared. "I have talked to Judge Roberts' clerk, Mr. and Mrs. Cristman. We regret your misunderstanding, but there is no way this hearing can be conducted today. Judge Roberts knows something of your situation and will consent to reschedule your hearing one week from today. However—" The officer peered at them imperiously. "However, by that date you must register and acquire your proper identification. You must realize that there is no way your petition for custody could be granted unless you abide by the most basic law of the land."

Sandy shrieked when she saw the three children scramble from the wagon. "Oh, thank God! Thank you, Lord. Frank!" she shouted. "Frank, Pam and David are back already, and the children are with them."

But by the time Frank had come running from the barn, Sandy's joy had vanished. David was glum as he lifted a trembling Pam to the ground. "I guess we should thank God, Sandy, but only for a respite. We haven't won."

"We have to go back next week," Pam sobbed. "We have to go back next week, and if we haven't taken the mark by then—"

Frank placed a strong arm around each of his friends as Sandy led them into the kitchen. "It's good news, Dave," he insisted. "The Lord is working or the hearing never would have been rescheduled."

Sandy ladled thick soup into bright crockery

bowls, but Pam pushed hers away. "No, thank you, Sandy. I'm not hungry."

Pam turned from Sandy to Frank. "I've been praying all the way home. There is no other hope. The court will take our children from us a week from today unless the Lord intervenes."

"Probably, Pam, but he will intervene. You have to have faith. You mustn't give up."

"I'm not giving up, Frank. But I have made a vow."

Sandy put a hand on her sister's shoulder. "God will hear you, Pam. I know he will."

"And you'll help me, Sandy. No arguments, no pressure?"

"I'll support you any way I can."

Pam stood and stooped to kiss David lightly on the forehead. "I've already talked it over with David. I've vowed to spend the next week alone, fasting, to pray for my children."

Sandy started to protest, but Frank interrupted. "Let her be," he said quietly. "Pam, Esther fasted seven days for Israel, and her prayers were wonderfully answered. Do as you feel you should. Sandy will look after the children, and we'll all pray with you."

"Thank you," Pam murmured, blinking back stinging tears. "I'm going upstairs now."

David gazed after his wife. "She's so trusting. She's so sure God will work a private miracle just for her."

"David, I won't change my mind and go downstairs." Pam gently pushed her protesting husband out the bedroom door the next morning. "Perhaps it isn't strictly scriptural, but I've made a vow to God and I will keep it. I will fast and pray until the hearing, and I know he will answer."

As David's footsteps faded, she spread the comforter over the bed. Then she knelt and burrowed her face into the softness.

"Oh, Lord, my God and my salvation, help me to remember your mercies and to trust you once more."

"Oh, Jesus, remember the little ones you love, and keep them safe, here, with us."

"Oh, God, be with David this week. He says he trusts you, and he knows it will be all right, but he's saying that to comfort me. Oh, God, give him your peace."

Pam alternately knelt, rocked, gazed from the bedroom window. Tears fell frequently as she pleaded for her babies. The sun completed its half-circle, and the moon rose. David knocked softly and entered to find her curled childlike in the bed. He undressed and lay beside her.

The next morning when he woke she was dressed, kneeling again near the window, sobbing softly.

"Pam, darling, I'm worried about you. I want to take care of you." He laid a hand on her shoulder, but she gently lifted it off.

"I must keep this vow," she sighed. "It's the only thing I can do for my children."

"I'll bring you some juice or some milk, maybe."

"No, David. Just a glass of water if you will."

"Just a glass of water!" The protest was only a

whisper, but the bedroom door banged as he let it close. "Is that all she thinks I can do about this?"

"No, I don't want any breakfast either!" he snapped, letting the kitchen door bang behind him. He picked up an ax and strode into the woods where a couple of fallen oaks still awaited cutting into firewood.

The ax rose over David's shoulder and fell into the hard wood.

Thud!

"Oh, God, why?"

Thwack!

"What can I do? They are going to take Pam's children from her, and all she can do is pray."

Crack!

"And all I can do is chop firewood."

On the third morning, Pam seemed sound asleep when David awoke. *At least she slept last night,* he thought. *Thank you, Lord, for that.* He tiptoed out.

She heard but lay still until the door clicked behind him. Then she opened swollen eyes, releasing the hidden tears. She turned her face into the pillow and tried again to pray. But the words she willed wouldn't come. No praise; no thanksgiving; no prayer for strength. Just one cry rising from the depths of her soul: *Oh, God, my children!*

David braced fence posts on the far side of the pasture. Slam! Slam! The hammer drove the nails far into the soft redwood.

"We could go away from here," he muttered to himself. "Frank and Joe could keep the place up, and Pam and I could take the kids and go up north, maybe, to their grandma in Eureka. But she has nothing. How would we feed and clothe the children?"

Thump. The fence held firm.

"They might not find us up at the Masters' place." No, that held too many ghosts.

Twang. The spliced wire was taut.

"Fight the authorities off when they come for them? They'd just keep coming back."

"I don't know which is worse, Frank," Sandy confided to her husband the next morning. "I stop at their bedroom door, and I hear Pam crying. But she tells me to go away. David disappears every morning and comes back in time for supper, his hands cut up from barbed wire. And I can't help either of them."

"No one can now but the Lord himself. I tried to offer Dave some hope, but he doesn't want hope. He wants answers."

"We're all praying for a miracle," Sandy reminded him.

"It will take a miracle. God says he won't let his children be tested beyond their abilities, but—"

"But sometimes, Frank, he has more faith in us than we have in him. He loves Pam and David, but, oh, how he's letting them both be hurt so. Oh, Frank, what good can come from this?"

The midpoint of the week was past. Pam woke with the sun on her face. She walked quietly to the window.

"Pam." David stirred, turned, and saw she was smiling. "Pam, are you feeling better?"

"Yes, David. I really, truly am. It's been a rough few days, but he's answered my prayers."

"I still haven't found an answer, Pam. I've considered moving away, hiding the kids, fighting back."

"David, it's going to be okay. I don't know just how, but I have peace about it now. I know whatever happens we'll come through, and so will Stephanie, Keith, and Beth."

"Then you're coming down for breakfast?"

"Oh, no." She even laughed. "No, I have a vow to keep and a God to praise."

His shoulders slumped again. *Why won't she let me comfort her?* he thought.

"Please, David, rejoice with me."

"I want to, but... I do thank him with you, darling... but I still need to know what to do."

David hoed weeds in the potato patch that day. He went over his options one by one.

"Flight? Starvation." The hoe rose and fell.

"Hiding? Temporary at best. They'd keep coming back, just like the weeds," he muttered.

"Fight? Defeat." He heaved a giant thistle across the field.

"Yield? No! I will not yield. I cannot see Pam lose those children."

As the sun lowered, David dropped the hoe and covered his face with his calloused hands. "It's the only answer. I must do what they ask. God, judge my motives; God, forgive me; I must accept the mark."

The day before the hearing, Pam still remained alone in her room. Sandy knocked softly, and gently opened the door. Her sister was silhouetted against the sunset.

"I'm ready, Sandy," she said. "I've given each of

them to God: Stephanie, Keith, Beth. And he's given me peace. Tonight I am going to sleep, and tomorrow the Lord is going with us to the court. And whatever happens there, I know it will be his will."

"Praise the Lord, Pam. He's already answered our prayers, just by comforting you. But," she concluded, "I believe he's going to keep your family together."

"Have you talked to Pam today?" Frank asked David at the supper table. "Sandy says she's much stronger."

"No," David snapped. "I haven't really talked to Pam all week. She asked me to leave her alone to pray, and I have." He shoved his chair back and stormed out the door.

Sandy gasped. Frank brushed her cheek with his hand as he stood to follow his friend into the twilight. He found him sitting on a log at the edge of the woods.

"Dave, don't shut us out. We want to help."

"Go help Pam with her prayers, Frank. I have to think."

"Dave, do you really think Pam wants to be alone tonight? You need each other."

David's face was turned away. "I can't," he muttered.

"Can't what, Dave?"

"Can't go to Pam. Good God, Frank, I can't face her. I can't stand to see her like this. Those children, they mean so much to her."

"And to you, Dave."

"I love them, Frank. I couldn't love them more if

I were their natural father. But Pam . . . it's my fault, you know, Frank."

"Don't be ridiculous, Dave. How could any of this be your fault?"

"It's my fault Pam never had a baby of her own. She wanted one so much." David stared past Frank, back to the old ranch house with its softly lighted windows. "We went to see a doctor just before the earthquake. Pam was fine. It was me."

"But, David, even if there was a problem, you can hardly blame yourself."

"If she'd married someone else she'd have her own children. She wouldn't have had to love someone else's. She'd have her own flesh and blood, and no one, not even the government, could take them from her."

"Dave, sometimes it's hard to see God's plan. But Stephanie and Keith and Beth needed you, desperately, and still do. It wasn't your fault, but it was his will that you and Pam not have children of your own. He was providing a place for these three precious ones. Don't you see that?"

"I see that my wife is going through hell on earth because she is about to lose the most precious things in her life."

"Sandy told me Pam's found her peace, Dave. Pam has accepted the Lord's will, difficult though it may be."

"Which means she believes he's going to perform that miracle."

"Not necessarily. I hope so. I pray so. But not necessarily."

David turned, then, to face Frank. "I've been over and over it this past week, Frank. There is no way God could choose to take those helpless little children from someone who loves them the way Pam does and turn them over to a godless, demonic government to raise. He wouldn't do that to them, and he wouldn't do it to Pam."

"I think you're right, Dave. I do believe that somehow you will be able to keep them."

"We will keep them." David's voice was suddenly firm. "It is God's will that Pam raise those children, and I am going to see to it that she does."

Both men stood, and David grasped Frank's arm briefly. "Now I do have some plans to make, Frank. Do you mind?"

Sandy, reassured by Frank, had gone upstairs to settle the children for the night. Then David slipped quietly in the front door. "That you, Dave?" Frank asked.

David stepped from the dark living room into the kitchen. He poured a glass of milk. "Frank, I've been thinking for a week, and I believe the Lord has shown me what has to be done. Will you pray for me, that he will give me the courage to do what I have to do? And that he will forgive me for it, if that is possible?"

"You know we'll pray for you and with you, Dave."

"Thank you."

David started to leave, but his determined words had frightened Frank. "David, wait a minute. Just what do you intend to do?"

"You'll know soon enough," he answered. He moved toward the door, but Frank blocked his way.

"David, I'm your friend. I'm your pastor. Please, David, tell me what you have decided to do."

David sat down again in a kitchen chair. "Maybe I should tell you, Frank, but you must promise not to tell anyone, especially Pam."

"I can't promise that, Dave. Pam's your wife, the children's mother."

"She mustn't know, Frank. Not until it's over."

David's sudden calm frightened Frank more than his earlier anguish. "Pam is as involved as you are in this, David. You have to share your plans with her."

"No. I don't have to share them with anyone. It's my responsibility."

"All right, Dave, I won't tell Pam."

"Or Sandy. Don't tell Sandy, either."

Frank reluctantly agreed. "Now, what are you thinking of doing?" But when David told him his decision, Frank recoiled in horror. "You can't! David, you must not. The mark of the Beast. Your own soul. No, Dave, I won't let you."

"I knew you would feel this way, Frank. But I've been praying for six days, and this is the answer. Nothing, even my eternal soul, is worth more than keeping those children with Pam."

David's hands were clasped as if to protect them, but his voice didn't falter. "I must register, accept the mark, and get custody of those children. Then, no matter what happens to me, Pam can raise them and protect them."

"Dave, no. You can't do this. Have faith. God will provide a way."

"He has, Frank, and this is it."

"No."

"Frank, I've accepted it. I'm ready. I'm only telling you this because I don't know what may happen to me. I think maybe it will cost me my life. And if it does, that puts a lot on your shoulders."

"David, if that happened they wouldn't let Pam keep the children anyhow."

"Frank, if something happens to me, you'll have to keep the authorities from knowing. You must keep them believing I am still here."

"But—"

"I know I can trust you, Frank. It's a tremendous responsibility to dump on you. You'll have Pam and our children, as well as Sandy and her boys to take care of."

"I'm not worried about that. I'm worried about you and your eternal soul, David!"

David chose to ignore Frank's plea. "I know you're up to the load, Frank. That's why I feel I can go through with this. I'll be leaving Pam and the children under your protection. God knows my heart. He knows I hate the Antichrist with all my heart. If it costs me my very soul, but keeps those kids with Pam, it will be worth it."

"I could knock you out and tie you up until after the hearing." Frank attempted a sick, rueful laugh.

"One, I'm physically strong enough that I doubt you could; and two, how would you explain that to Pam? No, Frank, I am going to do what I must."

David slept well that night, much to Pam's surprise and relief. *He really does feel at peace about this*, she reflected. *He trusts you, God, and so do I. Please*—she prayed before she, too, slept—*please don't leave us or the children.*

The entire household was up early. Stephanie, Keith, and Beth were excited all over again about the adoption hearing. David urged Pam to hurry with her dressing, telling her he had an errand in town before their appointment with the judge.

"What kind of errand?"

"Just someone I heard might trade some tools for a couple pounds of cheese." He shot a warning look to Frank.

Then, Jonathan and Mark came in from the barn with the morning's milk. "Mark," Sandy grumbled when her son reached out and turned on the TV. "Must we have that thing on this morning?"

"Sorry, Mom. Force of habit, I guess." He started to turn it off, but the announcer's words suddenly penetrated Frank's gloom.

"Wait," Frank demanded. "Listen."

"Oh, not today," Sandy groaned. Pictures of a reconstructed Jerusalem flashed on the screen, reminding her of events outside their circle. "Can you believe today, of all days, is the day they dedicate the new temple?"

The reporter continued: "In a surprise statement within the last hour, Secretary Crosetti has announced that he will personally attend the temple dedication. No further details have been made public. However, the secretary has requested that all but the most vital government offices and businesses be closed for the day, in order that the entire world may watch the dedication ceremonies."

Pam and David exchanged startled glances as the announcement concluded.

"The secretary will speak at precisely 10:00 A.M., Pacific standard time. We have no information as to the exact content of his speech, but it is obviously of utmost importance."

"Sounds like your hearing will have to be re-scheduled again," Sandy commented.

"Sounds that way, doesn't it?"

Only Frank noticed the tremendous relief in David's voice.

"**D**o you really think we should watch?" Pam asked quietly as the residents of the Cristman ranch gathered by the television set.

"The secretary requested that all citizens watch, and since the secretary requests, it just might be important." David sounded preoccupied. "We are citizens, or at least residents of this world, for the time being anyway. We need to know what he's up to."

"We're not citizens of his state, no matter what he says."

"Thank God for that, Sandy." Frank had addressed his wife, but he looked at David.

"Praise God," David agreed, fervently.

The TV cameras played on the floodlit exterior of the great stone structure. Scaffolding stood by the still-unfinished north wall. The stylized mural symbolizing the four-thousand-year history of Israel was barely begun. The temple stood, starkly primitive, built of hand-hewn stone and, because there were no more cedars in Lebanon, imported redwood timbers.

"Four years ago we wondered how it could possibly be rebuilt. The Arabs would never have permitted razing the Dome of the Rock. But God—"

"And the sacrifices, Joe!" Rachel had followed the resumption of animal sacrifice with intense interest, wondering how deeply her brother Aaron was involved. "Why, who could have believed that Jews would actually start killing animals and sprinkling their blood on the altar again?"

Frank shook his head in wonder as he responded. "We all had our pet theories, didn't we? And now we're sitting here in front of our television sets waiting to witness, what?"

"The unmentionable."

"Maybe, Pam," Sandy said, with a hint of a laugh in her voice. "Personally, I was counting my forty-two months from the comet, which would make this about six months early. . . but maybe."

"But if you count from the first big earthquake instead?" Joe did some quick mental arithmetic. "It would be just about right, wouldn't it, Pam? Frank, what do you think, or have you really not been counting?"

"I've counted from just about everything," he admitted. "The real keys should be the covenant with the Jews and the beginning of Brother Jonah's and Brother Elias's preaching, of course."

"But we never heard an exact date for the start of the preaching at the temple site," said Pam. "Remember, David, you wondered about that when we first began to hear about it?"

"Huh? What? Oh, I guess I wasn't listening."

"No matter, David," Frank commented. "We're just indulging in idle speculation while we await whatever we're awaiting."

"So we don't really know when the witnesses started preaching, and as far as the covenant with the Jews, Frank, there have been three or four treaties or pledges or whatever."

Frank nodded. "Exactly, Joe. There was one right after Crosetti revived, but there was also one right after the Thanksgiving quake. So, as I say, I've counted from several points. It is still," he reminded them, "idle speculation."

Their speculation was interrupted by a surge of martial music as the secretary's entourage approached the temple square.

"I see Brother Stan is right there, as usual," Pam remarked sarcastically, noticing that the secretary's favorite spiritual advisor shared Crosetti's spotlight.

"It's quite a crowd. I wonder if Aaron is there." Rachel seldom spoke of her brother, but her eyes searched the mob for his face.

The scene switched to the unfinished temple interior, revealing an astonishingly simple semicircular, theaterlike space. Folding chairs stood in neat rows facing what could only be described as a stage. A curtain of golden cloth hung from the domed ceiling; and in front of it, on a raised platform, stood a wide podium of creamy marble edged in gold.

Uniformed guards stood at attention along the

center aisle as Secretary Crosetti and Reverend "Brother Stan" Singer walked slowly toward the podium, arms lifted as if to bless the waiting crowd. Reverend Singer, who had always worn business suits and called himself Brother Stan, today wore pure-white clerical robes. The secretary also wore white—a military white, encrusted with gold braid. Both mounted the speakers' platform. Then, without explanation, the secretary was surrounded by several of his guards and ushered behind the curtain. Reverend Singer stepped behind the podium.

"Hush," Sandy whispered. "He's getting ready to speak."

Though the people in the ranch house kitchen were all certain the face they saw smiling and waving from the screen was the emissary of Satan himself, they were still too fascinated to move or speak as they awaited his words. Was it so strange that a godless world worshiped, literally worshiped, Singer's master?

"Thank you, my dear friends," the reverend began. He exuded charm, warmth, goodwill. "I cannot tell you how grateful we are for your cheers and your love. Ours has been a terrible struggle, repairing the damage our earth has suffered in the past few years. We have grieved as we buried our dead. Now we rejoice, as a strong, powerful worldwide government has brought peace and prosperity back to us. Now Lucio Crosetti and humankind have triumphed. How grateful we all are, you and I, that God has sent us a leader and deliverer."

"He makes him sound so noble, doesn't he?" Sandy mused.

"Able to deceive even, if it were possible, the very elect." Frank recalled again how close David had come to accepting the mark. "Who knows, really, who is safe from those two?"

The kindly voice went on. "It is truly a miracle that we can stand here, in this remarkable place, where God has been honored in so many ways under so many names. It is fitting that we should dedicate this place to a unified, purified faith in our Creator."

"Pam," Sandy gasped, "you were right. This is the revelation of the Beast, the Abomination of Desolation." They watched, mesmerized as the face in the plastic box continued.

"Many stories have begun in this land, stories of a God who created heaven and earth. That God, it was said, spoke to men. The stories even promised that God would send his very Son to enable humankind to reach him and be like him.

"Prophets came to the world—the ancient Jewish prophets, Confucius, Buddha, Jesus of Nazareth, Mohammed."

The camera moved in for a close-up as the smile faded. "But men have perverted and continue to pervert the messages of the Creator. Even now they oppose the common good, refusing to cooperate with the measures we have taken to restore order."

There was no sound in all the world as it hung on every word the man said. "Our great ruler has built this magnificent temple for the people of Israel, and for all the world, as a place to worship the true God.

But in the past weeks a few stubborn, ungrateful Jews have vandalized it. They have smeared the blood of sheep and goats on its beautiful altar."

Rachel was on the edge of her seat now.

"Men who call themselves Christians have so distorted the teachings of Jesus as to make him a false god. At present, handfuls of misled followers of Mohammed wage forays against our Middle East oil workers. We have tried to be tolerant of these religious fanatics, these who insist only their way is right."

"He's about to declare war," Frank said, taking Sandy's hand.

"These extremists hinder our growing prosperity. They are evil men, intolerant, claiming a monopoly on truth."

The crowd in the temple buzzed. The group at the ranch drew closer together; they held a collective breath as Reverend Singer paused for dramatic effect.

"Friends, brothers, and sisters, these few will no longer trouble us. Our deliverer has come, and his enemies are already defeated."

His audience cheered, and Singer raised his hands. "Quiet, my people," he purred. "Peace."

The circle in the kitchen watched, astonished, as thousands of people sat, trancelike, eyes fixed on the man at the altar. He smiled serenely once again.

"The time has come, my friends, to cleanse this world. But more of that later from our glorious leader. First, we dedicate this magnificent building, this holy temple."

The television cameras played on his pious face. "This is, indeed, a sacred occasion. The judgments of the past three years have been severe, but they are over. Now God has revealed, through this humble servant, that these troubles were sent to prepare the earth for the coming of God's true savior."

"Here it comes," Frank murmured.

The evil prophet had a beatific smile. "Many of you have guessed that the man whom I have served these past few years is no ordinary man. You know the deeds he has performed the past three-and-a-half years."

Frank glanced at Pam and nodded grimly.

"Do you doubt the hand of God in providing food and shelter to all of you in the face of unprecedented catastrophe? Do you question divine intervention in stopping the pillaging hordes out of the Orient? Do you recall how this man was pronounced dead and was restored in answer to our prayers, yours and mine? Yes, my children, these are the proofs that this man is sent from God."

The huge audience made no sound as Brother Stan went on. "I have been granted the profound privilege of giving to you God's ultimate revelation. The ancient prophets spoke of one who would rule from Jerusalem. Jesus of Nazareth did not claim to be that one—though his followers pressed him to do so— and he did not rule from here. But the promises were true. Yes, people of the world, your savior has come at last, sent from God to purge the earth of error and deliver you from God's judgment."

The heavy gold curtain was raised, and the crowd in the temple stared in stunned silence. Everyone in the Cristman kitchen gazed at the image on the screen, and then at one another.

Most had expected some type of religious shrine. Some had anticipated seeing Crosetti seated on a throne or wearing a crown. No one was prepared for this: Behind the brocade curtain, tall folding doors of dark wood and bright stained glass stood half open. A massive, elaborately carved desk and tall-backed chair with intricately tooled leather upholstery faced the waiting TV cameras and the bewildered world.

"An office," Frank muttered. "A sumptuous executive office. What in the world?"

The audience in Jerusalem began to murmur too, as Crosetti, escorted by uniformed guards, seated himself behind the desk. On the wall behind him were the trappings of the world's great religions: images of Buddha, the Hindu deities, the flag of Islam, the Star of David.

"A crucifix?" Sandy whispered. "How *dare* he include a crucifix!"

"He didn't dare use an empty cross." David and all the others in the Cristman kitchen felt a chill, a dark cloud that hid the bright spring sun.

In dark Jerusalem, Lucio Crosetti smiled his benign smile and waved to the cheering mob from his executive throne. Brother Stan motioned for silence. "As was prophesied so long ago, God's prince now rules from Jerusalem. He rules from this office, in this sacred place, because he rules by God's decree. The world will flock here to pay its homage and to receive justice from our leader, who will rule in wisdom and power, forever."

"How can God permit this? Shouldn't he strike them dead, now, for their blasphemy?"

"God has promised another three-and-a-half years." Frank's eyes moved slowly, first to Sandy's bewildered face, then to David's determined and steadfast face, and then to Pam's bowed head.

"Oh, God, three-and-a-half more years? For us?" Sandy asked. "God, help us all. For us, too, Frank? The three-and-a-half years?"

"I don't know."

The beatific smile still played on Crosetti's lips. He stood, hands lifted, and spoke into the microphones clustered on the desk. "Thank you, Brother Stan, for your faithful service in the past. We know you shall continue to teach the gospel to all mankind, revealing the truths that lie in all the world's religions. All these speak of me and of the God who sent me. Reverend Singer's message is one of love and hope. All who worship God, as seen through all faiths, will henceforth live in peace and prosperity."

The secretary's smile faded. "There remain, of course, a few who stubbornly insist theirs is the only path to God. These refuse to live at peace in the world, persisting in the path of self-will and intolerance. We have been patient with them, but no longer."

A collective gasp filled the ranch house kitchen.

"Now we begin to purge the world of the heresies that have plagued it. From this day forward, all will worship the god who dwells in this temple. Those who refuse to acknowledge my authority or to obey my words or those of my messenger, Reverend Singer, must be, and will be, neutralized. Then, and only then, this world will find peace." The secretary turned, bowed to the images enshrined on his wall, and left the room, with all the pomp expected of a god.

The television cameras moved outside to where Brother Jonah and Brother Elias still stood on either side of the main temple entrance. A reporter braved the mob to shove a microphone in front of Elias.

"Did you hear Brother Stan's speech, Preacher?" he mocked. "He's revealed that the secretary, and not your Christ, is God's deliverer. What do you think of that?"

"I am not surprised. God foretold in his Word that such a Beast would come and would do such things. But he who trusts God shall be saved."

The mood of the crowd was threatening as the camera moved to the other evangelist. "Jonah, were you expecting this too? And do you still think your Christ could rule better?"

"My Christ is God's only Son. This man receives his power from Satan. He is already defeated."

Crosetti had apparently remained in the temple, but the false prophet stood at the temple entrance. "You heard our leader. We must destroy his enemies, beginning here and how. Stone them!"

The mob was howling, roaring, and yet the false prophet's words were heard, somehow. Individuals here and there began to pick up pieces of stone from the base of the unfinished building. The reporters dashed for cover; but the two men, who had begun preaching there the day the Dome of the Rock was destroyed, stood firm.

Brother Elias held his Bible high in defiance as the first stones were hurled at him. Brother Jonah, too, lifted his hands. The retreating microphone caught the last words he uttered before he was struck forcefully in the back of the head. "The Spirit bears witness to the true Christ."

The stoning took ten minutes at most. The world's self-proclaimed Messiah then emerged from the temple, and the mob drew back to watch his departure. A functionary gestured toward the bloody corpses to have them removed. A reporter captured the ruler's harsh retort. "Let them lie. Let everyone see what happens to those who defame the name of Lucio Crosetti."

As John, the beloved disciple had foretold two millennia before, a worldwide holiday was declared to celebrate the murders of the two who had dared denounce the Antichrist.

There would certainly be no adoption hearing before next week.

"You can stop worrying, Frank," David assured his friend. "I'm back to my senses. If the children are taken from us, and if they must live through the next three-and-a-half years, they will be in God's hands. That man, that Beast, will not separate me from my God."

24

Three days later, on Sunday morning, Pam and David Cristman, Joe and Rachel Stenberg, Frank and Sandy Thomsen, and their children gathered for a worship service at the old ranch house.

The official word was out. All who refused to acknowledge Lucio Crosetti's authority were to be hunted down and sent to re-education camps. Those who refused to pledge allegiance to him would die, just as the evangelists in Jerusalem had.

As a reminder to any stubborn believers, the two battered bodies still lay where they had fallen. Crosetti, it was said, had ordered them to be left there, permanently, as a memorial. And he had decreed they would not decay. Skeptics who muttered that they had merely been sprayed with some kind of preservative did so in whispers.

As Frank finished his opening prayer, the group

was startled to hear a knock at the door. "Have they come for us already?" Rachel shuddered, hugging little Daniel close to her.

But Pam found Peggy Braden on the porch. "Peggy, come in. It's wonderful to see you, especially today."

Pam steered Peggy to a cozy rocker. "We were just starting our family devotions. We're so glad you can share them with us."

"Perhaps we should stop a moment," Frank said gently. "Peggy, we are all glad to see you, but what brings you out here? Has something happened in town?"

"You do know about the killings, don't you?"

"We know about the killings in Jerusalem. Have there been killings here too?"

"Not yet, Dave. But there have been arrests. They're knocking on doors, asking questions, checking our hands."

Everyone turned away, afraid to look at hers, as she extended them, palms open. "No, I couldn't. I was going to, once, but then when I went to the registry, the stylus was broken. And I thought about it some more. Then, when that creature stood there and claimed to be my savior, I knew I couldn't do it. Thank God for that broken stylus."

David and Frank looked at each other, then back at Peggy, who continued. "It was a terrible thing to do, even to consider. But God didn't let me go through with it. That does mean he forgives me, doesn't it?"

"Yes, Peggy, I think it does," David said. "Peggy,

no one but Frank knows this, but I decided to take the mark too. I had my reasons."

"No!" Pam screamed. "No, you couldn't. Darling, you couldn't."

"I'm sorry, Pam. I didn't tell you because I knew you would stop me if you could. I was going to do it in order to keep the children. But God stopped me too. I didn't have enough faith to trust God about possibly losing those kids. I was going to openly disobey my Lord. But then Crosetti closed the offices."

"They will take the children, I guess, when their celebration is over," Pam said.

David saw the pain and resignation in his wife's eyes. "Maybe, but now I know God is more loving than I had ever imagined. No matter what happens, he will protect us and the children."

Pam was quiet now. She took David's hand. "We'll make it through, David. You and me and God."

Peggy was crying, and Sandy stroked the older woman's hair as she might have one of the children's. "It will be all right, Peggy. Stay here with us. The Lord is with us. I know he is."

Frank hesitated, but it was important. "How is Tom doing, Peggy?"

"He is lost, Frank. I don't know how. I don't understand how any Christian could turn his back on the Lord so completely; maybe he never really believed. But I know he doesn't now. He gloated when . . . when that wretched man called the secretary the savior. He gloated! He said he was on the winning side and, if I wouldn't join him, I could get out. So I did."

There was no more to be said. Frank bowed his

head once more to thank God for Peggy's faith and her safety. Then he picked up his notes and began to preach to his tiny congregation.

"Praise the Lord. I know it sounds trite, even ritualistic, but praise the Lord that we are here, together, still believing in his power and his goodness. Most of the people out there can't praise him because they don't know him. They believe the one who has been openly revealed as the Antichrist is what he claims to be, God's savior. Or they admit he is the Antichrist but say he has won the final battle against our Lord. They call us fools for believing and traitors for living our faith."

Peggy, who had heard those very charges herself in the past few days, nodded at Frank's words.

"There is no one here today who has not reread the book of Revelation in the last three days. There is no one here, I dare say, who is not convinced that the two witnesses of chapter eleven now lie dead on the temple site, just as God foretold two millennia ago. And there is no one who does not long to understand what is going to happen next."

He looked at Sandy and the boys, his own family now, and at the friends who were as dear as any family could be.

"I want to offer you hope. As I calculate it, the witnesses in Jerusalem died just about three days ago. Late tonight, our time, I firmly believe God will raise them from the dead and take them into heaven. Perhaps I shouldn't say this because it is only a hope, a possibility."

David nodded now, recognizing the hope Frank

held out to them. "Will the final trumpet sound then?" their pastor asked. "Will God call us all at the same time? Maybe. Dear Lord, I hope so."

"But," he forced himself to remind them, "we have built up hopes before, based on our own interpretations of the Scripture. Daniel's prophecies tell us that another 1,260 days are decreed for Jerusalem," he warned, "and we all know they will be a terrible 1,260 days."

He continued reluctantly: "Starting today, the world is going to see the pouring out of the vials of the wrath of God, and the next forty-two months will, I believe, make the last forty-two look like our idea of heaven."

The little group drew closer together. "I wish I could tell you our trials will be over in a few hours. I wish I could tell you that when the Lord calls his two witnesses into heaven, the seventh and last trumpet will sound, and we, too, will meet him in the air."

"Amen," David murmured.

"Maybe. But perhaps we still have work to do on earth. Perhaps God's mercy will still be available and sufficient for the remaining time, and we must do his will on earth for a little while longer. All I can offer to you, my beloved friends and family, is the promise that he *will* come. Maranatha. Amen."

The words echoed back to him from each member of the little circle. "Maranatha. Amen!"

Epilogue

It was early morning in Jerusalem. Aaron Levy and some of his friends huddled in a back room in the tangled warren of the old Jewish Quarter.

"The Secretary says his guard struck all over the world at dawn, our time," Moise was recounting. "He says they rounded up all the trouble-making religious fanatics and sent them to detention camps."

"Well, he missed us," Aaron snorted. "He missed us, and there were about ten of us keeping vigil right there at the temple in plain sight."

"Has anyone other than Christians disappeared?" someone asked.

"I'm not sure. The official term is *religious fanatics*, but I've only heard specifically of Christians," Moise explained. "Aaron, tell us again exactly what you saw."

"We were there, at the Old Wall, keeping vigil,

and a large group of Christians were praying near the two bodies not a hundred yards from us. There were no soldiers. I'm sure of that. We would have seen and heard them. All we heard was that one strange sound, like a very fine trumpet, clear, resounding. Not blaring, mind you. It was very loud, but beautiful."

"And the light," a companion interposed.

"Yes, the light. It was so bright it may have blinded us momentarily, but only momentarily."

"Could it have just been the rising sun?" Moise asked.

"It was brighter than any dawn I ever saw, and it was gone in an instant. And so were the two corpses and all the Christians."

"An instant?" Moise persisted.

"An instant! I looked at my watch to be sure I hadn't dreamed the whole thing."

"The Secretary says they have the two bodies hidden away because the Christians said they would rise from the dead, just as they say their Jesus did."

"But how could they hide thousands, tens of thousands, of people?" This from Moise. "And if they had the bodies, or all those Christians, wouldn't the best proof be to bring them out and let everyone see them?"

"Mmm?" Aaron remembered something Rachel had said about Jesus. *If the Jews had hidden His body, why didn't they bring it out and stop the Resurrection story right there?*

On the other side of the world, where it was night, a television set droned on in the old ranch house near Little Valley. Government spokesmen continued to explain away the mass disappearance of those religious fools who had persisted in defying Secretary Crosetti.

But there was no one there to listen.

ABOUT THE AUTHOR

Jean Grant was born in Michigan, but has lived most of her life in northern California. She earned a bachelor's degree from the University of California, Berkeley, and has worked for more than thirty years as a clinical laboratory technologist. She has never married.

Her articles and short stories have appeared in such publications as *Evangelical Beacon, Mature Living, Home Life, Seek,* and *Power for Living.*